DOMESTICALLY SOUL TIED BY MARY GORE

DOMESTICALLY SOUL TIED

Remember To ThinkPink Publications, Master Publisher

Copperas Cove, Texas

rttp.publications@gmail.com

MARY GORE

DOMESTICALLY
SOUL TIED

An Urban Tale of Survival

DOMESTICALLY SOUL TIED

MARY GORE

This book is dedicated to all the Harmony's and Rashad's in the world.

Shared trauma does not equal compatibility.

DOMESTICALLY SOUL TIED

PROLOGUE

November 19, 2000 was a cold, rainy day for the Jones household. Mrs. Kelly Jones was set up to deliver a baby girl later that day.

On the way to the hospital, Kelly and her husband Edward had been playing slow jams all morning, trying to get her in the mood for her delivery.

The song "Summer Rain" playing melodically on volume 23 was soothing for Kelly, taking her mind off all the contractions that were coming every 15 minutes. She noticed as the rhythm of the song played her baby girl kicked to every beat. By the time she made it to Saint David's Hospital she was in full-blown labor.
At 3:45 pm Harmony Alise Jones was born.

She had the prettiest eyes you'd ever want to see, and she had a head full of thick, curly black hair.

Doctor Henderson held Harmony up and was about to place her in her mother's arms. Within seconds of opening her eyes, Harmony glanced up and her first gaze was that of her mother's beautiful face.

Kelly looked down for a moment, locking gazes with her beautiful baby when suddenly a surge of pain shot through her chest.

Dr. Henderson immediately noticed her face contort with pain and pulled baby Harmony back from her mother's arms just in time.

MARY GORE

Kelly's face turned blue and she stopped breathing. The delivery had gone from beautiful to tragic in seconds.

The doctors immediately rushed Edward out of the room and baby Harmony was transported to NICU.

Edward was devastated. How can what had begun as the most beautiful day of his life end up being the absolute worst? Harmony would be their first child and he had never experienced anything as beautiful as watching his wife give birth.

At 5:42 PM, Kelly Jones was pronounced dead due to cardiomyopathy.

The news was unbearable for Edward. All the staff and people visiting other patients' hearts went out to the heartbroken man who was screaming and crying in the middle of the lobby.

The nurses tried to calm him down by reminding him that he still had his beautiful baby girl to care for and that she needed him.

Overwhelmed with grief, Edward left the hospital a few days later.

A week after coming home, Edward buried his wife. She was put away nicely in a beautiful gown and the chrome casket was covered in pink hydrangeas, her favorite flower.

The Pastor preached a beautiful sermon telling the Jones family that, "God does not make any mistakes" and that the church would help them with anything they needed.

The choir sung and the eulogy was read.

DOMESTICALLY SOUL TIED

Kelly's mother Martha couldn't help but to notice the distance between Edward and his newborn Harmony. He had not held her once during the service. Although he'd lost his wife, Kelly's mother still wanted him to understand he still had a daughter in this time of grief.

After the funeral and the repass, Ms. Martha stayed to help Edward with Harmony. After she put Harmony to sleep, she sat quietly on the sofa next to Edward.

She didn't know what to say, but she had to find the words. She was hurting too. Kelly was her only daughter.

Swallowing back tears, she reached for Edward and said softly, "Baby I know your hurting. You have every right to be, but a piece of Kelly is still here. She wouldn't have wanted you to be here hurting."

Edward broke down into tears and sobbed, "She was my comfort; her heart beat matched mine. How can I live without her? All she wanted was to make me happy. There's something you might not know…"

Edward's voice was filled with tears as he looked at Ms. Martha who held an eerily strong resemblance to his wife.

"I forced her to have that baby," he said lowly as tears began to flow from his eyes.

"That baby is your daughter," Ms. Martha replied, "The same heartbeat you heard was the same one Harmony felt every day for nine months. You haven't touched or looked at her since she was born Edward. The child hasn't even been here a week and already lost her mom on the same day she was born. You had years with Kelly, Harmony only got to see her mother once."

MARY GORE

Martha reached for Harmony who was sleeping like an angel in her bassinet beside the couch. She placed the baby in his arms and told Edward to look at his daughter.

More tears fell as Edward turned his head crying viciously.

Martha coaxed softly, "Baby I know It's hard, but look at your daughter. If you cannot do it for Harmony, do it for Kelly."

Placing Harmony directly in his eyesight, Martha said firmly, "Kelly was *my* daughter. She was stubborn as an ox! If she didn't want this baby, she would have never had her!"

As soon as Edward looked at Harmony, she locked eyes with her dad. He was so upset over the past week he forgot how pretty her eyes were. They reminded him of Kelly.

Baby Harmony blinked at him twice before staring in his eyes. Edward began to dry his tears. He pulled the baby to him telling Harmony how sorry he was for not being a father. As he rocked Harmony to sleep, he vowed to always be there for her no matter what.

DOMESTICALLY SOUL TIED

CHAPTER ONE

Eighteen years had passed by and Harmony Jones looked more and more like her mother each day. She had long, thick hair that framed her gorgeous face. Her chestnut skin glowed and her eyes were hazel with flecks of blue.

Everyday her father Edward drove Harmony to school. They would start off each day with the song, "Summer Rain." Edward played it each morning just to see his daughter smile and sing her mother's favorite song.

Every time he dropped Harmony off and she'd wave, he'd feel a lump in his throat. A piece of his heart would ache because he knew her mom would have been crying everyday waving goodbye.

With a final wave, Harmony rushed off to find her girlfriends and bounded up the stairs. He still could not believe what a beautiful young lady he'd raised.

Edward drove to work in happy silence, thinking of his daughter. He was the manager at the local Ford dealership.

Everyone who knew Edward pretty much had the same opinion of him. He was a nice man who'd help anyone in need.

Edward had vowed to stay single after his wife died. He kept his heart only for Kelly. He felt that was the least he could do since she'd died having his daughter.

MARY GORE

It saddened him that his daughter was growing up and would probably go off to college soon, then eventually find her own husband and start a family.

His thought was cut short as he heard a bit of commotion in the front of the dealership.

He noticed a woman with three kids standing in the lobby. She was scolding one of the kids for something and trying to talk to the clerk at the desk at the same time.

He noticed she held the vehicle loan application in her hand that had DECLINED stamped across. He also noticed she wasn't wearing a wedding ring.

He could tell she was struggling, trying to discuss the application and keep her eye on her kids. As he got closer, he noticed her eyes were wet; like she'd been crying.

"Hello, may I help you?" Edward asked.

Startled, she looked up. Edward was jolted by how much her eyes reminded him of Kelly's and was momentarily startled as well.

The woman was embarrassed. Here she was crying like a wimp while this man stood there to assist her.

She quickly cleared her throat and asked for the manager.

"I am the manager," Edward said with an amused grin. "My name is Edward Jones. And yours?"

"I'm Zoria Anderson," she said and held out her hand.

"What seems to be the problem today Zoria?" Edward asked softly.

DOMESTICALLY SOUL TIED

Zoria didn't know where to begin. Edward understood the look on her face and motioned her to go into his office on the left.

Edward walked in his small but handsomely decorated office. It had oversized leather furniture and a huge desk that was neat and organized.

Zoria sunk into the chair in front of him and the words seemed to tumble out of her mouth.

She told Edward that she was going through a divorce and had been put out in the cold with her children by her abusive husband.

Edward listened in disbelief. He couldn't stand men that put their hands on women.

Zoria began to cry as she explained that she had no money or a job and was trying to get a car on credit, but her husband had blocked her from all their assets.

Edward slid the box of tissue to her and gave her a moment to gather her composure.

"Zoria, you don't have to cry. I can help you."

Edward buzzed his secretary and had her bring the keys to one of the Certified Used cars they had just gotten into inventory.

Zoria didn't know what to say. "I promise, I usually don't ask anybody for anything," she said honestly. "I don't know how I'm going to pay you for the car, but I promise that I will."

MARY GORE

Edward assured her that he would give her some time to get on her feet and it was the least he could do to help a sister out.

He didn't know why, but he felt compelled to help her. Here was a single woman with two sons, 18 and 9, and a beautiful brown-eyed 5-year-old daughter, who by now had fallen asleep in her mother's lap.

"I understand your pain. You made the right decision to leave with your kids," Edward said.

Zoria filled out some paperwork for Edward, gathered her children, and shook his hand before leaving.

Edward noticed how soft her hands felt when her son unexpectedly threw his arms around his waist thanking him for helping his mom.

When they shook hands goodbye, Zoria instantly felt at ease. There was something about the real concern she saw in his eyes that made her feel comfortable. She quickly assessed that he wasn't wearing a wedding ring either.

Two weeks later Zoria drove back to the dealership. Ever since he'd met her, Edward couldn't stop thinking about her.

He kept telling himself he just wanted to make sure she was okay, her having a crazy ex and all. He shook his head and stared back down at the huge mountain of paperwork on his desk.

Hearing a soft knock at his opened office door, Edward looked up to see Zoria.

DOMESTICALLY SOUL TIED

She had on a pretty yellow dress that accentuated her curves perfectly. Her hair was pulled back in a loose ponytail and her shoes and purse were vivid yet flattering.

"Hello Edward," she said softly. She was pleased to see the look of appreciation in his eyes as he looked up at her and broke into a grin. He was trying hard not to let her see how happy he was to see her.

"I just wanted to stop by and thank you again and tell you how much my children and I appreciate you. The car is working great."

"You should be proud of yourself." Edward said sincerely. "You were the one who had the strength to walk away and stay away."

Zoria smiled brightly and said, "I'm feeling stronger these days. Well, thanks again," she said as she turned to leave.

"Zoria," Edward said quickly, "I don't mean to be forward but do you want to join me for lunch? I was just about to wrap things up here and have a bite to eat."

Zoria was flattered and agreed to meet him a few blocks over at his favorite jazz restaurant near downtown.

As they were being seated, she heard the harmonious sound of Louis Armstrong playing in the background. Edward noticed her swaying slightly to the music playing and asked Zoria what she knew about him!

She chuckled, "That's right up my alley. My favorite song is "*A Kiss to Build a Dream On.*" That song is therapy to my soul."

MARY GORE

When the two were seated, Edward could not stop staring in her eyes.

"I don't mean to be rude, but I just had to compliment your eyes," he said quietly. "They remind me of my late wife's Kelly, she had eyes just like yours."

Zoria began blushing explaining to him that she got her eyes from her great grandmother. She immediately felt guilty for blushing, but she also didn't know what to say.

She thought she'd lighten the mood and looked at him and asked, "By the way, what's your wife last name because I truly don't want to be sitting next to my cousin-in-law."

Edward couldn't help but to laugh. He was intrigued by this hazel-eyed vixen. "Oh, wow you have jokes, don't you? Just like my daughter, little Harmony."

"Harmony is a beautiful name. How old is she?" Zoria asked?

"She's about to turn 19 in two months, I been raising her all by myself since she was a week old."

"I'm so sorry," Zoria said sincerely, "May I ask how your wife passed?"

Edward shook his head yes and took a deep breath. "She died during childbirth. My wife Kelly was a beautiful, healthy woman. I met her in eighth grade. I knew she was the one when I saw her. She couldn't stand me at first, of course," he chuckled, "but as years went by, we grew from classmates- to friends, then from best friends-to dating, and soon as I graduated out of high school I made her my wife. I didn't want to wait to have children, but Kelly did. As always, she wanted to make me happy, so on our first-year anniversary, Kelly stopped taking her birth control. I didn't know she was giving in to my wants. We'd used condoms since we'd become sexually active, and I thought maybe she'd started taking the pill. At first, I was finally happy that I got to feel the real feeling, but two months later Kelly got sick and I found out she was two months pregnant. I guess I was so excited on the first night of not having to wear protection, I made it count." Edward's voice trembled slightly as he thought back to one of the most beautiful times of his life. He continued, "Fourteen appointments, seven breast-feeding classes… we went by the book on everything. The day her contractions started everything was perfect until she gave birth to Harmony. Within two hours after delivering our sweet baby girl she passed away.

Zoria began to cry softly, "I'm so sorry. I can't imagine how terrible that is. I apologize for making you relive that…"

Edward replied warmly, "Zoria, you're okay. I wasn't trying to turn our lunch date into a counseling session but this the first time I was able to talk about it in 18 years without crying."

She smiled as she grabbed his hand and looked him in his eyes. She commended him on raising his daughter alone.

"Thank you. I learned a lot, but when it came to the feminine stuff, she had to call on her grandmother!"

They both chuckled. Finally, the waiter came and took their order. They spent the rest of their lunch talking about lighter subjects, finally ending on one they were both well-versed on; their children.

MARY GORE

Speaking of children, Edward looked down at his watch and noticed the hour and a half had flown by. He forgot it was Wednesday, Harmony's early-out day.

"I'm so sorry Zoria, I would love to stay and talk all evening, but I'm running late to get my daughter. I forgot she gets out early on Wednesdays.

Shocked Zoria asked, "Today is Wednesday? My son Eric does too." She jumped up from the table and gathered her purse and sunglasses.

Edward, delighted they had so much in common asked her, "Does Eric attend St. Martin?"

"Yes, he does."

"My Harmony does too."

They both smiled and Zoria decided to exchange numbers with Edward hoping that they would have another chance to spend time together to talk some more. It felt good having adult conversation with a member of the opposite sex.

Leaving the restaurant, Edward walked Zoria to her car and noticed she had a flat.

She immediately began to panic because she was already running late. Edward insisted that he bring her to get her son since he had to go to the same place to get his daughter.

When they were in the car Edward called his dealership to come fix the tire and to drop the vehicle at her home when it's done.

DOMESTICALLY SOUL TIED

Zoria, who was used to her sorry ass ex-husband was impressed that Edward knew exactly what to do. She wasn't used to men like this.

She smiled to herself and sat back as they drove off to scoop their kids.

MARY GORE

CHAPTER TWO

"Damn Harmony where your fine ass daddy at?" Iesha asked popping her gum.

"Girl please," Harmony said rolling her eyes. She laughed at her friend. All her friends had a crush on her handsome daddy. "Iesha, you know my daddy's coming, but on second thought, he's never late. I tried to call his phone but no answer I hope everything is OKAY."

Harmony was beginning to worry when Iesha elbowed her.

"Look Harmony! There goes Eric's fine ass."

Harmony laughed. Iesha thought everybody was fine. "Ain't nobody worried about no Eric he ugly anyway."

Iesha yelled, then whistled, getting Eric's attention to walk over.

Harmony was exasperated. "Why'd you do that, Iesha? Now his ass gone come over here."

"Say friend come here," Iesha said, ignoring Harmony.

"Who me?" Eric asked.

Eric approached the girls, walking nonchalantly although he was a little nervous because he secretly has a crush on Harmony.

"Man, Iesha why you do shit like this?" Harmony hissed.

DOMESTICALLY SOUL TIED

"Girl hush you know you like him to hell. Now look bitch, smile and act cute don't embarrass me hoe."

Sometimes Harmony couldn't stand Iesha's mouth, but she loved every bit of her. She and Iesha had been friends since elementary. While Harmony was no angel, Iesha could cuss with the best of them and was the epitome of a "Dare devil" with her ghetto ass.

Harmony felt her face getting hot as Eric sauntered over.

"Hi, did one of you ladies call me? Eric asked.

Before Harmony could say no Iesha burst out with the songs from a rap song, "Fuck all that radio shit my home girl trying to get that- *black biggie biggie black ah hah"*

"Iesha!" Harmony yelled.

Eric couldn't help but to bust out laughing, singing the rest of the song with Iesha.

"What you know about music like that Eric?" Harmony asked surprisingly.

"What you trying to say Ms. Harmony? I honestly thought music like that would be too hood for your taste."

They stood there and stared at each other.

Iesha suddenly said, "Damn I'm sorry, so its fuck me now huh?"

They both laughed at Iesha who pretended to be annoyed. She turned facing them both, but looked at Eric and said, "Oh you slick like her ass too, huh Eric? Well, don't worry about me because the both of ya'll can watch this ass walk away."

MARY GORE

As soon as she left, Harmony told Eric she was sorry for how Iesha was acting.

"Don't do that. Don't ever say you're sorry. You can apologize to someone but never be sorry."

Harmony looked Eric directly in his eyes, and for a moment her judgment of him changed.

They heard the honk of a horn and turned to see Harmony's dad driving up.

"I'm sorry Eric that's my dad I'll see you tomorrow."

As she approached the car, she noticed a woman in the front seat.

"Wait, is that my mom?" Eric asked Harmony. Harmony stood there in disbelief. In all her 18 years of living she had never seen her dad with a woman; let alone one riding in the front seat of his car.

Edward got out of his vehicle and gave Harmony a big hug.

She whispered in his ear, "Dad who is this, and why is she riding with you?"

"I'll tell you later, get in baby girl," he said as he walked her to the car, opened the back door and kissed her on her forehead.

Eric who was just as confused asked his mom what happened to their car.

"I had a bad flat tire son and Mr. Edward offered to take me to pick you up so you wouldn't be late."

Eric noted that "Mr. Edward" was the same man that helped his mother by giving them the car two weeks ago and broke into a grin. He gave Edward a big hug and thanked him for helping his mom.

"We didn't have nothing left and because of you we have hope."

Harmony went from confused to agitated and said, "I'm lost! So, everybody knows each other except for me huh? Bet!"

Eric entered the car with his head down. He was so happy to see Mr. Edward so that he could finally thank him, he didn't realize he spilled the tea on him.

The drive to Ms. Zoria's house was quiet.

"We're here," Edward said.

"Thank you so much you are a good man!" Eric said, giving Edward a fist pump.

"For sho' big dog!" Edward chuckled.

Eric looked down at Harmony, "Goodnight to you as well I'll see you tomorrow."

Harmony didn't even wave goodbye to Eric. Instead, she sat in the back seat disappointed. The look on her face said it all.

"Good night Zoria I'll call you tomorrow. Let me know if ya'll need a ride in the morning. I'm available, but your car should be here later tonight."

Eric and his mother waved goodbye and headed inside.

Edward prepared his self for the drive home. He knew Harmony was upset. When he got in, he asked Harmony if she'd like to ride upfront.

MARY GORE

"Naw' I'm straight." Harmony said with an attitude.

"Why are you mad at me, what did I do wrong?" Edward asked his spoiled daughter. He hated to see her like this.

"Dad I'd rather not disrespect you today, so your best bet is to just drive this car," Harmony said defiantly.

"Disrespect me how? I have always allowed you to speak your mind."

Harmony's legs began to shake, and tears welled up in her eyes. "Dad, how dare you have that lady in our car? Why was she riding with you anyway?"

"Harmony, her tire went flat she needed a ride."

"Bullshit!" Harmony screamed.

Edward yelled back, "Why are you acting like this?"

"You must think I'm stupid or something!" Harmony continued. "I heard you say that you will call her in the morning which means you already have her number. On top of that Eric even knew you. I can't even believe you would do this to my mama."

"Your mama??" Edward got mad, "All I ever been doing for you is what your mother would have wanted me to do. It's been over 18 years. I haven't even touched another woman let alone talked to one. It's been only me and you for years. I got to move on baby, your mother died years ago and I haven't done anything in those years."

Harmony looked up and said jealously, "So now you're saying you love this hoe?"

DOMESTICALLY SOUL TIED

"Where is this coming from? Harmony why you are talking like this?" Edward asked in disbelief. "I'm done!" Harmony yelled, "Take me home!"

Edward turned around in his seat and started his engine and began to cry. As the tears rolled down his face, Harmony kept her head down, knowing that she had crossed the line. She knew she was being petty and unreasonable, but she didn't want to share her father, not at all.

A couple red lights and a few turns later, Edward pulled on the side of a cemetery. Harmony looked up and when she finally realized where she was, she began yelling and begging her father to take her home.

Edward opened his car door politely and took Harmony's hand.

Harmony's eyes were red, and her throat was sore from crying. She, nor her father, had ever been to her mother's grave.

They walked inside the cemetery. Edward's hand shook as he held Harmony's. Three turns and a left led them to Kelly's grave.

Harmony stood at her mother's grave. She never wanted to see it, but her dad said it was time.

Edward cried out "Kelly I don't know if you can hear me, but I need you. I need you to forgive me. I pushed you to have a family and when you did you lost your life. A part of me died the day you did. There were some days I didn't want to eat; some days I couldn't even sleep, but when I looked in our daughter's eyes, I saw you. She gave me a piece of you to hold onto and I have held on for as long as I could. A few weeks ago, I met a lady in need of help, she

MARY GORE

was divorced and had nothing left. She has three kids and they didn't have anything. Her husband abused her and when she asked for a divorce, he took it all. I helped her get a car and I took her to lunch today. I like her I never felt anything since I lost you, but I've been a great father and all I want to do is feel loved again I'm so empty inside."

Edward's voice broke as he poured his heart out at his wife's gravesite.

Harmony stood there looking at her father. She had never realized nor had even thought about how hard it was on him. She knew that he tried to make her life full of love while dealing with grief in his heart himself.

Harmony ran into her father' arms and cried, "Daddy, I'm sorry. I just thought if you met someone you would forget about me."

"Harmony I would never do that to you I love you," her father said.

The look on his face was filled with love and for the first time she felt complete.

It started raining and they both ran back and got in the car Harmony jumped in the front seat and ask her dad to forgive her.

"I already did," Edward replied.

Harmony turned the radio on and to her surprise "Summer Rain" was playing. They looked at each other and that was the confirmation they both needed. They drove off smiling.

DOMESTICALLY SOUL TIED

CHAPTER THREE

Zoria and Edward dated for a while. They were enjoying each other's company and companionship and were constantly surprised at how much they had in common.

Edward felt like a schoolboy again. Now he had more of a reason than just Harmony to get out of bed in the mornings.

Just as quickly as their relationship began, almost overnight it ended.

One night, Edward's phone rang. It was Zoria.

Smiling, he picked it up and answered, "Hey beautiful."

Zoria, on the other end of the phone was devastated. Edward had been nothing but good to her. A good friend and listener. He'd helped her through one of the toughest times of her life, but she couldn't lie to him.

Her ex had been calling every night. Zoria was torn. She had never heard her ex talking like this. He had made so many changes. He had even started going to church.

Zoria felt she owed it to her children to be with their father. She grew up without her father and vowed she would never allow her children to be raised without theirs.

Now she was confused. While she liked Edward, she had spent the last 20 years with her husband. Yes, he was abusive, and he drank, but everybody deserves another chance.

MARY GORE

"Hi Edward," she said, her voice trembling. "I should be telling you this in person, but I'm too much of a coward."

Concerned, Edward sat up and became serious. "Zoria, what's wrong?"

"Nothing and everything. I don't know how to tell you this, but I have been talking to the kids' father every night for the past few weeks. I have decided to give him another chance."

Edward was stung, but not surprised. Being alone all these years allowed him to study people. He'd heard that women from abusive backgrounds will keep going back to their source of pain several times before they finally leave.

"Zoria. I won't lie, I'm disappointed. I hadn't even thought about dating or being with another woman until I met you. I took it slow because I didn't want to rush you. I had hope that you would go back. You deserve so much more."

Zoria felt like the wind had been knocked out of her. She knew that he was telling the truth. She knew she deserved more, but the guilt she felt speaking to her husband was unbearable.

He was in church now and always telling her that divorce was not acceptable in God's eyes.

Besides, dating Edward wasn't easy when they had two teens who were also close.

She and Edward had discussed the sparks they saw between Eric and Harmony.

It was all too much. Ultimately, Zoria made her decision. She was going to be a good wife and mother. She was going to show her husband that she would never leave him as the other people in his life had.

Making the announcement to her children wasn't easy. They were just getting used to having stress free days without constant screaming and violence.

Surprisingly, they took it a lot easier than she thought they would. Even though her ex was crazy, he loved his children. Zoria was glad she hadn't been intimate with Edward. This made leaving him alone much easier.

MARY GORE

CHAPTER FOUR

"Good morning Harmony," Ms. Johnson, their school secretary said brightly. "I'll be so happy when ya'll graduate! You and your friend Iesha. These two months isn't going by fast enough. Speaking of Iesha- here she come now Lord let me get into the office before she spots me."

"Ms. Johnson! Hey boo don't hide now! What you say about me?" Iesha drawled.

Ms. Johnson responded sincerely, "I simply said to Harmony how I was going to miss the two of you when ya'll leave."

"Aww how sweet! But the Holy Ghost is speaking Ms. Johnson! It's telling me that you just tired of being bothered with us!" Iesha replied.

Ms. Johnson laughed and told them to get to class before they were late.

Iesha caught up to Harmony, "What up Harmony where your fine ass stepbrother at? The one you can't do-but want to do- but if you did-that would be nasty?"

Harmony burst out laughing. "Girl you crazy. I told you, we're just friends. Besides my dad and his mom are just friends. My father told me that Eric's dad came back in the picture and his parents been talking about making it work.

DOMESTICALLY SOUL TIED

My daddy and her only went out on a few dates but they decided to just remain friends still."

Harmony still felt a little guilty about how she reacted when she saw her dad in the presence of another woman for the first time. She hoped he found someone else soon.

"Shid, so what you are saying is your daddy fine ass isn't cuffed yet?" Iesha asked sticking out her tongue.

Harmony rolled her eyes, "Girl bye! My daddy does not want your ass!"

"Bitch I'm just playing you couldn't handle me as your step mama anyway!" Iesha's face grew serious, "But for real, how you been? I know you been trying to get that scholarship for some time now."

Even though Iesha was ghetto as hell, she was her true friend and really cared about her. "They told me I'd hear something next week," Harmony answered trying not to seem nervous.

"Well keep me updated hoe love you, you know us players got to play the game like chess, but we gone always have to checkmate a nigga because they be trying to play!"

Harmony laughed and walked into her third period class.

"Good afternoon Harmony, about time you decided to show up," Mr. Henry said loudly, "there was a note just sent by the principal requesting you to immediately come to his office."

This sounded serious. "Damn, Iesha" Harmony thought to herself, "I know her ass was gone get us in trouble."

MARY GORE

Harmony walked to the principal's office. As she approached the secretary's desk, she noticed two police officers standing in the hallway staring at her.

Ms. Johnson, what did Iesha get us into now? I can't afford to get in no trouble…" Harmony began to explain.

Ms. Johnson had tears in her eyes and a look on her face I'd never seen. Principal Franklin walked out his office and joined she and I at the desk.

"Harmony, I'm afraid I need you to come into my office. These officers are going to join us, and your grandmother is on the way."

They walked into the principal's office where Harmony was seated. Principal Franklin sat down behind his desk, and two officers walked in and introduce themselves.

"Good morning Harmony, my name is John, and this is my partner Mark."

"Hello," Harmony replied, "but my question is why do you want to talk to me?"

They asked her if she knew someone named Charlie. Harmony told them that she didn't. Then they asked if she knew a lady named Zoria.

"Yes, I do she has a son named Eric and he's my best friend."

The officer continued his line of questioning, "So, may I ask when the last time was you saw Eric or his mother Zoria?"

Harmony noticed the little black book the officer was writing on.

"May I ask a question officer? Why are you taking notes and asking me these questions shouldn't my parent be here?"

Well Ms. Harmony the questions I'm asking pertains to a case that is under emergency investigation. It is vital that we have a time frame so can you please tell us when the last time was you spoke to Eric.

"It was a day ago, he texted me and told me his dad came back home to work it out with his mom and he didn't want to be at home with him."

"How did you know his mother?"

"Her and my dad used to talk for a little while, but they decided to be only friends. I still don't understand why I'm being questioned about my dad relationship status. Mr. Franklin can you call my dad for me because it just doesn't feel right?"

As soon as she'd said it, Harmony's grandmother walked into the office with tears running down her face.

"What's going on Grandmother?"

She noticed her grandmother eyes were swollen and red. Harmony stood up to greet her grandmother, whom she was happy to see, but not sure why she was seeing her.

Ms. Martha looked over at Mr. Franklin and asked, "Have you told her already?"

"Told me what?" Harmony asked.

Ms. Martha told Harmony to take a seat and she gave the officer'ss permission to tell her.

MARY GORE

The officer looked at the young girl and cleared his throat and began, "At 9:32 this morning, my partner and I responded to the crime scene at the Ford dealership. One man by the name of Charlie drove his ex-wife Zoria and her three children ages 5,9, and 18-year-old boy named Eric up to your father's job. He thought your dad was seeing Eric's mom because he found text messages between the two of them in her phone."

"OKAY, so where is my dad and what does that have to do with them?" Harmony asked.

Harmony's grandmother told her to let the officer finish and stood next to her with her hand on her shoulder.

Officer Mark finished, "Mr. Charlie pulled Zoria and her children out of the car forcing them at gun point to enter the dealership. Once inside the dealership he walked into your father's office, waving the gun around demanding that your father admit to the relationship. When you father told him there was none he got upset and shot his 5-year-old daughter in her neck.

He asked again for the truth when he didn't get the wanted answer, he shot his 9-year-old in the head."

Harmony was trying her best not to scream. She began shaking her legs as this horror story unfolded in front of her.

"Your father pleaded with him to let him prove that Zoria and he were only friends, but when he aimed the gun at your dad, Eric jumped in front of your dad trying his best to protect him but sadly Mr. Charlie pulled the trigger...killing Eric.

DOMESTICALLY SOUL TIED

He then told Zoria and your father to get on their knees and face one another. He shot and killed them before turning the gun on himself resulting in taking his own life."

The officer had been on the force for years. He had never seen such a violent end to a domestic dispute. He tried hard not to let his personal feelings get involved with work, but this was just a damned shame.

"I'm so sorry young lady here is my card we will have someone to contact you tomorrow, I know this is a lot, but we are here if you need us," he said softly.

Harmony hands were locked to the arms of the chair and her legs shook violently. Her eyes were blood shot red. Ms. Martha grabbed her granddaughter as the others left the office.

Harmony hadn't said a word, until she yelled, "No!"

She began throwing things, hitting the desk, punching the walls. All her grandmother could do was allow her to let it out. Harmony dropped to her knees numb, afraid, broken and shattered everything she loved died.

Ms. Martha began to pray. Harmony was so hurt. She began vomiting everywhere. Ms. Johnson and the school's nurse came in to help Martha clean up Harmony and get her off the floor.

Harmony fell into her grandmother's arms and wept bitterly.

"Let it out baby you've been holding it in for too long," Martha said. She had lost her daughter and now her son-in-law. He was just as much of a son to her as any of her birth children.

MARY GORE

"Why Lord?" Harmony yelled, "Why did you take my mother? Why did you take my father? My best friend?"

Ms. Martha held on to Harmony, "Baby I know you hurt, but don't get mad at God."

She looked at her grandmother in disbelief.

"How can you pray to someone who took your daughter and you still say Lord thank you? I'm done! Fuck this! Fuck this life, I hate everybody!"

Ms. Martha continued to hug her granddaughter because she knew deep down inside, she was just broken. Lord help us she prayed silently rubbing Harmony's back.

DOMESTICALLY SOUL TIED

CHAPTER FIVE

The black stretch limousine lined the sidewalk among the row of cars of close family. The smell of fresh picked roses, black gowns and suits filled the downstairs of her father's home.

"Come on Harmony!" her grandmother yelled, "The limousine is here to take us to the funeral."

As Harmony looked in the mirror she broke down in tears. I must be some horrible joke. Everything attached to me is ripped away.

Harmony barely heard the words of the Pastor. She was determined to sit through the funeral and not lose her mind.

"Today we are gathered here for the untimely death of brother Edward. He was loved by everybody he knew but most of all he was known for his love to his beautiful daughter Harmony."

The same pastor who spoke at her mother's funeral when she was just a baby was preaching at her father's. The Pastor mentioned her dad as being a hero who would never give up.

"If anyone wants to say something about brother Edward the floor is open," the pastor continued as Harmony squeezed Iesha's hand.

Harmony looked around the church, before anyone could stand up Harmony let go of Iesha's hand and stood up.

MARY GORE

"I do," Harmony said.

Everyone picked their head up. Ever since the tragedy, everyone knew Harmony hadn't said one word.

"Good afternoon everyone. My father was a good man I never knew how much I loved him until he was gone. This is the same church that buried my mother when I was only a week old. Now instead of celebrating my 19-birthday next week with my father I'm burying him today. Not one person in this room can imagine the pain I feel on today."

Harmony looked down at the casket and continued, "Daddy I love you. Grandmother, I love you, but I can't don't this anymore."

Harmony dropped the microphone and ran out of the church. Ms. Martha ran outside to catch her, and Iesha followed.

They finally got Harmony calm enough to get back to the family's home for the repass.

When everyone had left the repass, Martha walked upstairs and knocked on Harmony's door. When she didn't get an answer, she entered her room. A letter was left in an envelope on the bed.

It read:

"Dear Grandmother,

I'm OKAY I need time to think I'll be back Sunday I just need some space I love you, but this is very hard for me.

Love, Harmony"

Ms. Martha sat on the bed letting out the tears she'd held back for so long.

DOMESTICALLY SOUL TIED

She cried out, "Lord I need you right now! I know Harmony is mad because I've been in that place before, but she really needs you more now than ever please keep her safe!"

Sunday morning came, and Harmony arrived back at the house.

"Hey Grandmother, sorry I went to my friend's house to get some fresh air. I am OKAY now. We will be OKAY," Harmony said. She hoped she hadn't worried her too badly.

Ms. Martha stood there confused because she knew God would hear her prayer but that was quick!

"You sure baby?" her grandmother asked.

"Yes Grandmother, I am. I'm going to take a bath and I'll be back so we can go get something to eat. I'm starving."

Harmony walked upstairs and prepared her bath. She was about to knock on the bathroom door to make sure her father wasn't there, and then it finally hit her.

She began crying uncontrollably. The thought of her dad's funeral, Eric's smile, and everything that led up to this point. She wanted desperately to know what was running through her dad's head in those last seconds of his life was overwhelming.

Ms. Martha knocked on the bathroom door, "Harmony open up sweetheart. Let me help you."

No answer.

"Harmony, can I come on in?"

Harmony still didn't reply.

MARY GORE

When her grandmother opened the door, she saw Harmony crying in the tub.

"Harmony, baby you must let this out or you are going to kill yourself with grief."

"I never got a chance," Harmony kept saying it over and over.

"A chance for what?" Martha asked.

"I never told Eric I loved him, and I never got a chance to tell my dad thanks," Harmony cried.

"Harmony he always knew you were thankful, and I know Eric loved you too. It's time for you to start your healing process. I love you and we will get through this together."

Martha combed through Harmony's hair and she began to hum her mother's favorite song.

This was supposed to be one of the happiest times of her life. Her birthday and her high school graduation were this year's biggest events. Harmony didn't want to celebrate her birthday nor her graduation because they were too painful to spend it without her dad.

A month later, the day they been waiting their whole life for.

"Happy Graduation day girls!" Martha yelled proudly to her granddaughter and her best friend. She was extremely proud of her granddaughter for making it to graduation even though she wanted many times to quit school.

"We made it hoe!" Iesha yelled to Harmony.

"Girl watch your mouth! Don't you see my grandmother right there?"

DOMESTICALLY SOUL TIED

"I forgot that quick! You know how my mouth is girl! I'm so proud of you honey everything you've been through. You continued to keep pushing and striving. Many would have given up, but not my Harmony! I can see us now walking the halls on Presley University. Four years with my best friend I can't wait!"

Harmony forgot to tell Iesha she didn't get accepted to the university they both applied for, but she didn't want to ruin the moment.

"OKAY girls time to smile on a count of three say cheese and cheddar biscuits."

"Naw' scratch that Ms. Martha! I've got this one!" Iesha laughed, "Harmony what's comes at the end of every good sentence?"

 They both looked at each other and yelled "Period Pooh!"

That moment was a big accomplishment for Harmony as she walked across the stage to get her diploma. Although she didn't see her father in the audience, she knew his spirit was there.

MARY GORE

CHAPTER SIX

"Well Harmony this isn't Presley University, but this community college is going to have to do," Martha said as she pulled up to the campus.

Ms. Martha couldn't understand why Harmony didn't want to go anywhere else. When her dad died, he only had a $20,000 insurance policy to cover funeral cost and something for Harmony, but she could have gone to a better school than this one.

After paying the taxes, and funeral cost she decided to buy herself a 2017 black hellcat she named "The Bat Mobile." He also left the house in Harmony's name.

As Ms. Martha kissed Harmony goodbye, she cried; leaving red marks on her cheeks.

"Alright Grandmother," Harmony said. Out the corner of her eye she saw a guy staring at her, and Grandmother was cockblocking.

"I love you Grandmother," Harmony said a little softer.

"I'll call you later and be safe," Martha replied. Although she would only be two hours from the college, she feared leaving Harmony.

As Harmony walked to her dorm a voice yelled, "Excuse me queen!"

She turned around and noticed it was the same guy that stared at her earlier.

DOMESTICALLY SOUL TIED

"What this look like chess to you?" Harmony responded walking faster.

"No ma'am but it seems like you do need a king in your life," he said.

"I hear you. How I can help you sir?" Harmony said dryly.

"My name is Rashad, what's yours?"

Harmony couldn't help but to stare at his big arms, and beautiful big eyes.

"I don't give that kind of information out to people I don't know," Harmony said sarcastically.

"Look baby girl, I was only trying to get to know you I didn't mean any harm."

"Well now you do, goodbye Ronald," Harmony said with a big smirk on her face.

"Girl you funny. It's Rashad, remember that," he said as he watched her walk away.

Harmony walked away switching and blushing hoping he was still watching her.

Harmony soon settled into college life and the first semester passed by quickly. She would call and check in with Iesha and they would stay on the phone for hours exchanging stories about their colleges. Her conversations with Iesha were the only things that offset her boring college life.

Harmony was on her way to the dorm when she spotted Rashad's fine ass. She had seen him around a few more times since she first met him, and she liked his swag more and more.

MARY GORE

She couldn't understand why she was so attracted to him. Instead of speaking she went to her dorm and decided to give Iesha a call.

The phone didn't even ring once before you heard Iesha's loudmouth, "Bitch I'm up here with all these lame ass people! I need to come over there by you hoe."

"Girl it's only been one semester! You have to give them people time because you a lot to handle at once!" Harmony replied.

"Whatever! How the dudes look up there? All the ones that keep hollering at me have names like "Luther" and "Arthur" I need me a damn "Tyrone" or "Darnell.""

They both laughed at that, then suddenly Harmony said, "Speaking of dude's Iesha, there's this fine ass dude that tried to holler at me my first day here. I been seeing him around campus, but I can't man."

"How do he look? Is he my type or fuckable or your type?"

Harmony laughed, "Girl Iesha, sometimes I wonder how in the hell did you get in that university with a mouth like that."

"You really want me to tell you how my mouth got me in here?" Iesha said acting nasty, "All I did was open wide and said ahhhh…"

They both laughed at that.

"On some real shit Iesha, this nigga is everybody's type. He's tall and chocolate."

"Bitch you talking about Hershey or Godiva?" Iesha interrupted.

DOMESTICALLY SOUL TIED

"Bitch both!" Harmony screamed, "Not only that, his muscles, beard, abs, shoulders, and lips; I bet his insides are made of chocolate butter…"

"That man can't be that fine, and you didn't jump on him?"

"Girl, that was my first day here, I didn't want to seem desperate."

"What did he say when he tried to holla at you?" Iesha asked. She always liked details.

"He was like hello queen, and I told him do I look like a chess board to you."

They laughed some more, and Harmony told her the rest of the story and how she ended up walking off calling him the wrong name.

"Bitch, you stupid, how dare you. I'm over here suffering, and you got Mr. African calling you queen and you playing childish ass games. Girl that could have been your husband, all I wanted was for you to drop some of the pictures in my box after. You lucky I got exams in the morning, because I would have been cursing you out the whole night."

"Love you Iesha," Harmony said, happy that she shared about Rashad with her girl.

"Love you to Queen," Iesha joked.

"Girl bye!"

The next day as Harmony walked to class, she heard a deep, familiar voice say, "Excuse me Queen."

She tried to act surprised like she didn't know the sound of his sexy voice. He was standing there dripping in chocolate sweat, and on top of that she could see his print through his boxer shorts.

"Let me guess Ronald, right?" Harmony said, following Iesha's advice, trying to be a little flirtatious.

Rashad blushed and instantly she could feel her blood pressure rising.

"It's, Rashad. I haven't seen you since the first day of school."

"I have a lot of classes and I'm rarely out," she said.

"Look, I normally don't do this, but can I take you out?" Rashad asked shyly.

"You don't even know me, why you want to take me out anyway?" Harmony asked.

"Let me tell you the first day I saw you, you had on a pink shirt, with some jeans. Your hair was long and pretty, judging by your nails, you seemed to be a happy person because you had them painted pink. Most of all, when I looked in your eyes, they reminded me of rain. Some people hate rain I love it."

Harmony could feel the connection, but she couldn't understand why. She had never been talked to like this by a man before. It was scary and exciting.

"I'm not trying to run game on you, I simply just would like to take you on a date that's all," Rashad said hopefully

"My name is Harmony," she said to Rashad… "And I wouldn't mind staring into your eyes all night…" she said to herself.

DOMESTICALLY SOUL TIED

"Here is my number, text me when you make it home, and I'll see you tonight Ms. Harmony."

"Maybe you will maybe not Mr. Rashad."

Harmony walked off hoping that this time he was still staring. She counted to five and when she finally turned around his eyes pierced her heart. She spent the rest of the day thinking about him, but she didn't want to seem desperate, so she figured she would wait till the next day to text him.

The next morning, she decided to text him:

"Good morning."

She was so nervous to even look at the phone to see his response. Not even a minute later, he texts a response:

"Good morning Ms. Harmony."

She blushed at the thought that she didn't include her name and he already knew it was her.

"What are you doing today, if you don't mind can I take you on a date later on tonight?"

They agreed to meet for their date later that night. Harmony jumped up trying to find something to wear for the date. All she had were jogging pants, sweatpants, and dingy t-shirts. She had a wig in her closet, some athletic shorts, and a shirt that showed her skin. While she was digging in her closet her phone started ringing, it was Iesha. She had to be in class in a few minutes. She didn't have time for this shit!

Harmony hurried up and answered, "Hello…"

"Damn hoe you done dumped me again, why you sound like you aggravated?" Iesha asked indignantly.

MARY GORE

"Iesha, girl I am frustrated! Do you remember the guy Rashad I told you about?"

"Who? My chocolate prince? What about him?"

Harmony told Iesha how she'd ran into him yesterday; dripping in chocolate sweat. She described what he had on: basketball shorts that were pulled down just enough so that his pelvis line was visible. Then to top it off he had on a white beater that should his muscles.

"…and when he smiled…" Harmony continued, "I almost fainted. I was so nervous trying not to stare, but it was obvious that he caught me off guard. He asked me on a date, and I told him yes. The crazy thing is I don't have no clothes."

Harmony broke down. As much as she wanted to go on the date, she just couldn't let him see her in that manner.

"I tell you what hoe, I'm your hood fairy godmother today," Iesha said cheerfully.

"Iesha, I have to be in class in 30 minutes. How can you help me from there?"

Iesha assured me she could help me. "Harmony, you are going on this date just get to class and I'll take care of it. Call me when you get out of class!"

"Thanks girl!' Harmony said.

Harmony packed her bag and headed to class.

Finally, classes were over for the day. Harmony was so ready to get out of class and back to her room to see what Iesha had planned.

DOMESTICALLY SOUL TIED

She dropped her books on the floor and jumped right in bed to call Iesha. As soon as she pressed call Iesha was facetiming her on video.

"Hey, girl what you come up with?" Harmony asked.

"I got my cousin Myra headed over there now to help you."

Harmony stared at the phone looking confused because for as long as she's known Iesha, she had never heard of a cousin name Myra.

"Girl where you get a cousin name Myra from? I swear your ass have the most kin folks that never been kin."

"Bitch you stupid," Iesha blurted out, "but for real Harmony Myra my cousin I sent her some money she got your outfit, some hair, shoes, bras and some panties because I know you haven't bought any lately, perfume and more."

"Damn Iesha, how much I owe you?"

"Girl I did that for us, you're not gonna embarrass us like that, that man sound too fine for you to be acting childish. I bet he big huh?"

"Iesha!" Harmony yelled. "I'm not like that. You must have forgotten I'm still a virgin."

"I forgot about that girl; you know how I like to get excited especially when chocolate is in the mix. You need to go ahead and take your bath; she'll be there in a few minutes. Call me when you get out." Iesha said before hanging up the phone.

As soon as Harmony got out the shower, she heard a knock on the door.

MARY GORE

It was Iesha's cousin Myra. When she walked in, Harmony couldn't help but to notice how beautiful she was.

"Before I get started what time is your date for and where are you meeting him at?" She asked straight business-like.

"My date is at 8:30, and he wanted to meet me at the cafe."

Myra spouted off her next set of orders, "Text your date and tell him you will be meeting him for 9:15 pm and instead of meeting at the cafe tell him to meet you by the water fountain."

"Why would I meet him at the water fountain?" Harmony asked, not sure she liked being told what to do.

"You new here huh?" Myra asked. "Meeting a dude at the cafe is like being claimed. You don't want everybody in your business, plus if it doesn't work out you can walk to the café and show out anytime."

"Thanks for telling me that cause girl I wouldn't have known," Harmony said feeling like she'd dodged a bullet.

As Myra started opening the packages, she asked Harmony if she'd ever worn make up. When Harmony told her that she hadn't, Myra could hardly believe it.

"Girl why? Your mother must not have liked you wearing makeup."

"My mom died when I was born, my daddy raised me."

"Did your dad ever dress you up?" Myra asked incredulously.

"Nope. Once he ordered me a beautiful dress three months before prom, but someone killed him a month before I went." Harmony was still not used to saying those words out loud.

"Shit, that's messed up. Well honey when you see yourself on tonight the heavens will awake."

An hour later Myra was finally finished.

"Done!" She said proudly.

"Let me Facetime Iesha," Harmony said reaching for her iPhone.

"Um no. You need to see yourself first," Myra said convincingly.

"Yeah, I guess you right girl," Harmony said.

Myra grabbed the mirror and told Harmony to close her eyes and not to peek. Harmony stood there shaking in her seat.

"One two three Viola!"

When she opened her eyes, she couldn't believe what she saw. Tears began to fall she jumped up hugging Myra.

"Girl don't cry you're gonna make me cry, and besides you are going to mess up your makeup!"

"This is beautiful Myra, these lashes oh my God!" Harmony exclaimed.

"Girl you know I had to hook you up with them good lashes, they're called "Troublemakers" because that's exactly what you're going to be doing tonight! Causing trouble! If you like them, you need to shop with Plush Barbie and tell them Myra sent you."

MARY GORE

"Yes, girl, I will be shopping with them," Harmony promised. "Now can you take my picture? I have never saw myself like this. You did that!"

"Sure, I can," Myra said.

As soon as she snapped Harmony's picture, a message from Rashad popped up. Since Myra was taking pictures, Harmony told her she would call him after.

She called Rashad back and put him on speaker, because she didn't want to mess up her hair or makeup.

"Hello Ms. Harmony, I wasn't rushing you, but this lonely old frog been sitting by the fountain hoping my princess come kiss me and turn me into a prince. Obviously, that won't work because the girl I'm waiting for is a queen."

Harmony's heart melted, "I'm leaving now I'll be there in ten minutes Rashad."

When Harmony hung up, she noticed a strange look on Myra's face.

Myra asked her how long she had known him. Harmony admitted that she'd met him initially on the first day of school but went on to explain how she had been playing hard to get.

"Well girl, watch yourself these men are no good around here they will treat you, beat you, then leave you pregnant," she said looking down at her belly. Myra kept thinking the voice from Harmony's phone sounded familiar but...nah...

"Thanks for the advice. I didn't know you were pregnant; Iesha didn't tell me."

DOMESTICALLY SOUL TIED

"Don't even tell her girl, she talks too much," Myra said laughing.

"Anyway, I don't think Rashad is like that," Harmony said.

Myra eyes opened widely, "Rashad who?" Myra refused to believe the voice on the other end was her ex that left her in her current predicament. The fact that his name was also Rashad had to be a coincidence.

"I don't know his last name, but girl he is fine do you hear me. He's 6'2, chocolate, pretty teeth you have got to know him!" Harmony said, thinking about how sexy that nigga really was.

"Just watch him is all I can say, be safe and if he asks who did your makeup don't mention my name. Don't even tell him you know me please." Myra said, hoping they didn't know the same Rashad. She gave Harmony a quick hug before walking out the door.

Harmony couldn't help but to notice how her demeanor changed when she mentioned Rashad's name.

She knew she was running late so she texted Rashad:

"I'm five minutes away here I come"

Rashad:

"Okay just waiting on you beautiful"

Harmony had never been more nervous in her life than she was walking under that patio. She saw Rashad standing by the fountain with a red rose in his hand. They locked eyes as she got closer.

MARY GORE

"Ms. Harmony, I never thought I would ever see an angel, but I can say that I have tonight," Rashad said in his husky, deep voice.

Not only had Harmony never been talked to this way by a man, she'd never had a man look at her like that. She knew exactly what that look meant.

Wanting to keep things light, she said softly, "You clean up pretty well yourself. So, Mr. Rashad where are we going tonight?"

"Just follow me that's all you need to do," he said and grabbed her hand.

They walked through the parking garage holding hands. Rashad could tell she was nervous. When they approached the vehicle, Rashad went over to her door and opened it. A lady should never have to open a door.

Harmony was truly impressed because that was her father's philosophy. He closed her door, got in and started the car and began to drive.

They made small talk as they drove down the highway. She was starting to feel more comfortable with him.

"So, Ms. Harmony how did a beautiful lady like you find your way down here in these country woods?"

"Well Mr. Rashad," Harmony replied.

"Girl call me Rashad you act like I'm old or something."

Harmony laughed, "I was taught to respect my elders.

"Elders?" he scoffed, "Girl I'm only 25, by the way the question should be how old are you? I know you legal because you in college."

DOMESTICALLY SOUL TIED

"I'm 19 years old sir," she said still messing with him.

"Girl you're still a baby. So, what brings you to this college? You look like one of the Presley girl types."

"Well it's funny you said that. I was originally supposed to go there but I decided not to." Harmony figured she'd just leave it at that. If she told the truth about her reason for not going it would have messed up the date.

"Enough about me, what about you?" Harmony asked, diverting the attention away from herself.

"I've been living down here all my life. I work and I am in night school for business and marketing. What's your major? Have you chosen one yet?"

"I haven't figured it out I'm just doing basics for right now."

"Okay I understand," he said, "So, what do you do for fun everyday Harmony?"

Harmony told him that she was really a homebody and aside from classes she's usually at the dorm studying.

"Another day, another dollar," Harmony said honestly. She didn't have a social life at all.

Rashad couldn't help but to laugh, "Let me find out you a little hood and boujie! I might have to let you meet my grandma and tell her I done hit the lottery on my first pick!"

"Boy stop, I'm nobody I swear," Harmony said modestly.

Rashad stopped the car in the middle of the street. Harmony jumped and asked him what was wrong. He reached over, pulled down the mirror on the passenger side,

MARY GORE

and said, "Look. Look in this mirror Harmony, you are a beautiful black woman, own this. Look at your eyes, your lips, your mouth, man you are fucking gorgeous. Don't ever forget that."

Harmony could feel something stirring in the bottom of her stomach that spread like fire between her legs. She hoped he didn't know how he affected her. She calmly smiled and said, "Yes Rashad, I'll remember that."

He started the car and told her how ever since meeting her he couldn't get her off his mind and that there was a song that reminded him of her, and he couldn't get the song or her out of his head.

Harmony sat back curious as to which song he'd play.

"This was way before your time, so I know you probably never would have heard it," Rashad said as he plugged his aux cord into the radio and turned the volume up loud.

The moment Harmony heard the beat tears began to viciously stream down her face. She could not hold it in.

"Wait, what's wrong Harmony?" he yelled.

She immediately started having a panic attack, and within seconds she passed out right in the car with "Summer Rain" still playing.

CHAPTER SEVEN

Four hours had passed since Harmony's panic attack. When she finally opened her eyes, all she could see were bright hospital lights. Her grandmother was sitting on the sofa with the Bible on her leg. She tried to speak to get her grandmother's attention and realized her mouth was extremely dry. She tried to get her thoughts together. She was so confused about what happened.

Once her grandmother heard her stir, she immediately rushed to her bedside telling her to not speak.

"How did I get her and where is Rashad?"

"Is that his name? All I know baby is that you had a panic attack and passed out in some boy's car. It's a good thing Iesha tracked your phone because he didn't even know your last name. Iesha called me after she tried to see how your date went and after no response, she contacted me with the location."

"Where's Rashad?" Harmony faintly whispered.

Before she could answer there was a knock on the door and the doctor and his nurse walked in.

"Hey, kid my name is Dr. Andrews. I heard you gave a young man a scare on his first date," the doctor chuckled.

MARY GORE

Harmony held her head down in embarrassment. "It's okay," he said. "My question is, why haven't you been taking your anxiety pills?"

Instead of her being honest with the doctor and telling him she hadn't taken them since her father's funeral, she pretended like she had left them at home.

"Well if it wasn't for your date's quick thinking you probably would have lost a lot more oxygen than you did."

"Where is he doctor?"

"He is in the waiting room and has been here all night.

"All night? What time is it?" Harmony asked looking around frantically. She nearly freaked out when she found out it was 10 am. She had exams coming up and couldn't afford to miss any.

Despite her pleas, Dr. Andrews insisted that Harmony return to school in two days to give her body some time to heal.

"Thank you doctor she will follow your instructions," Ms. Martha said sternly.

"Speaking of this young man here he is," the doctor announced. As he walked out the door, Rashad's sexy ass walked in.

"Hello Harmony," he whispered walking to her bed side. "I'm so sorry baby, I was so scared."

Harmony asked her grandmother if she could give them some time alone and she reluctantly agreed.

DOMESTICALLY SOUL TIED

"What time is it?" Her grandmother asked the nurse. "I'll be back in 15 minutes." She said before rolling her eyes at Rashad and walking out the door.

"Harmony…," Rashad began.

"No, wait Rashad, let me say something," Harmony said, taking a deep breath, she continued, "When I was born my mother died. My father raised me until about four months ago. My dad was murdered trying to help someone out. He played "Summer Rain" for me nearly every day of my childhood because that was my mother and his favorite song. When you played it, I guess it caught me by surprise and I had a panic attack. "

Embarrassed and upset that she had to share all this heavy shit, Harmony held her head down.

"Dang mama," Rashad's voice was drenched in sadness. "Why didn't you tell me?"

"Rashad I was scared. I had just met you and I didn't want you thinking I was some charity case. I didn't even want to tell myself that this was real, but I must deal with it."

Rashad gently wiped the tears that rolled down her face.

"Harmony I don't know why God led me to you, but I do know that I'm never leaving your side."

Harmony hugged his neck and squeezed tight. For some reason she believed him.

He looked in her eyes he kissed her forehead and said softly, "I'm here for you."

MARY GORE

Downstairs, Martha was standing at the vending machine in the hospital cafeteria trying to decide what she wanted when she heard a familiar voice calling her name.

"Martha? Is that you? I couldn't tell if it was you at first, you seemed to have put on a few pounds." Diana Matthews said, walking up to her old nemesis.

"Hey Diana," Martha said dryly, "I see you still being shady after all these years. I haven't seen you in ages. How are you?"

They made small talk and Martha asked Diana why she was at the hospital.

"My granddaughter is in the hospital." Martha said.

"Wow, how old is she now?" Diana asked. When Martha answered "19" she was mad that she still looked good for her age.

"You know my grandson Rashad is 25 now. His mother MaryAnn ran off with a man 25 years ago and I ain't seen her since and he hasn't either."

"I'm so sorry to hear that Diana," Martha said sincerely.

"Girl we are okay honey! Ain't nothing God can't do. I'm just up here trying to find my grandson. He took my car last night and went on a date with some girl. Martha, you wouldn't believe this, but her little hot ass passed out in my car. She was probably on drugs or something. You know how these new girls are nowadays!"

She hadn't got the sentence finished before Martha bumped passed her and walked off, "Excuse me, Diana I have to go make sure my drug using, fast ass granddaughter is doing better."

DOMESTICALLY SOUL TIED

Diana stood there with her mouth wide opened. Ms. Martha was so mad she couldn't think.

"Hey, excuse me sir, you got to go," Martha said suddenly, bursting into the room.

"Wait, Grandmother what happened?" Harmony had never seen her so angry.

"Little boy your grandmother is looking for her car and for you downstairs. I suggest you find her. Matter of fact, make sure you tell her Martha said this and I got damn quote: this girl right here," she said pointing at Harmony, "will never be MaryAnn."

Rashad immediately let go of Harmony's hand, walked out and slammed the door.

"Rashad!" Harmony yelled, "Grandmother what did you do? Who is MaryAnn? Is that his girlfriend or something, tell me?"

Martha took a deep breath and looked at her granddaughter. She knew she was getting older and eventually would have to let her grow on up. "I went to school with his grandmother. She had a drughead daughter named MaryAnn, who had a son name Rashad. She left him with his grandmother Diana when he was a baby. I don't like his grandmother, or her drug head ass grandson."

"What does that have to do with me, or how you just treated him? So, you really gone hurt her grandson with words like that? I'm about to go!" Harmony said angrily and got up to get her things together.

"Where the hell to?" Martha yelled just as angrily. "Harmony you not going to date that boy. Leave him and

MARY GORE

his bitter ass grandma in the gutter where you found him at."

Harmony stopped turned and whispered angrily to her grandmother, "You're just as bitter because your daughter left you too, and you've been alone ever since."

 She turned a ran after Rashad trying to see which way he went and left a stunned Martha standing there who couldn't do anything but cry.

DOMESTICALLY SOUL TIED

CHAPTER EIGHT

"Rashad!" Ms. Diana yelled when she saw him walking fast down the hall.

"Man, Grandma lets go," Rashad said angrily.

"Wait Rashad why are you so upset?" Diana asked her grandson.

"Man, some bitch upstairs just brought up my mama. Who is she?"

"Don't pay her no mind. She just doesn't like you because your grandfather used to date her in school. We were friends, but when she left for college, he didn't go and ended up marrying me. Don't pay her no mind. Let's go and I'll explain everything in the car."

When they entered the parking garage and walked to the car, they turned to hear footsteps running toward them.

"There you are!" Harmony yelled. "I been looking all over for you."

Rashad brushed passed her like she didn't exist.

"Come on Rashad, leave that girl and her punk ass grandma alone," Diana Matthews said coldly.

Harmony stood in tears, "Really Rashad, I thought you said you were never going to leave my side."

MARY GORE

He tried to walk off and avoid looking at her, but in his heart, he knew she needed him.

"Rashad, please talk to me, don't do this," she cried.

Diana looked at Rashad and said firmly, "I'm going to tell you one last time, let's go."

Rashad got in the car and stared straight ahead. Diana looked at Harmony one last time and said, "Tell your grandma this one here is going with me too. You ain't the right one for him anyway." Then drove off.

The ride home was quiet. When Diana finally pulled up to her house, Rashad couldn't help but to wonder how Harmony was feeling. She seemed so helpless when she was sick.

"Man Grandma, why you have to be so mean to her?" He asked suddenly.

"It was her grandmother that started it!" She said defensively.

"Yeah whatever," Rashad shot back, "How you gonna let her talk about your daughter like that?"

Diana was hurt. "You mean my daughter, the one that abandoned you? I could have been living my life but no, I had to raise you. I was done raising kids. Your punk ass daddy just had to have your mama all to himself. They didn't even want you!"

"Grandma," he interrupted her, not wanting to hear any more.

DOMESTICALLY SOUL TIED

"No, you shut up Rashad, I've been being quiet for too long. I haven't even spoke about your sperm donor, or your unfit ass mother."

"Grandma, please stop." Rashad begged. He was building up with anger and rage.

"Sometimes I wish I just could have a do over. If I could I would have swallowed your mother whole and pissed her out." Diana spat the words out like venom.

He couldn't even believe his grandmother was talking like this to him. Rashad's eyes filled with tears.

"Wipe your face. I don't need none of my church members asking me about my household. You're a man but sitting here ready to cry. That hoe done made you real soft. Your new name is going to be Cream Puff. Now come on and take me to bible study hell." Diana huffed to herself, "This boy done got my blood pressure up Lord help me!"

When Rashad pulled up at the church his grandmother asked if he was coming inside. The look on his face gave her his answer so she told him that she'd be finished with Bible study in two hours and she'd meet him back in front.

Rashad shook his head and told her he wasn't coming back to get her.

"What do you mean? Child, here, I got two dollars, go get something to drink because you need to calm down," Diana said trying to hand him money.

"Naw' Grandma, I'm straight. I don't need anything from you," he said through clenched teeth.

Diana was becoming impatient. "Rashad take these two dollars boys you're so selfish!"

MARY GORE

"I'd rather live on the streets, then to stay another night with your bitter old ass. I'll be by tomorrow to get my things. Take this old beat up ass car anyway." Rashad said as he cut the car off and slammed the door. He threw her her car keys and walked off. Diana had never seen him this upset.

DOMESTICALLY SOUL TIED

CHAPTER NINE

Harmony was laying across her bed in tears when suddenly, she received a text from Rashad:

"Where you at?"

Before she could respond he called her phone. "Hey Rashad, I'm in the dorm."

"Can I come over?" he asked.

Harmony kept telling him that the dorm was closed, and she was under a curfew, but he told her that he needed her.

"Fuck them folks, come here now."

Harmony looked down at her phone. A part of her didn't want to risk getting caught but the other half said go.

"Okay Rashad, send me your location I'm on the way."

Before he hung up, he told her to bring some clothes because she was staying with him tonight. She jumped up, packed some clothes, and headed out her dorm.

When Harmony pulled in the location she wanted to gag. She could smell the strong scent of old urine in the air. The location he sent was in the projects.

"I'm here" she sent a message Rashad.

He texted back and told her he'd be out in ten minutes.

As soon as she put her phone down, she noticed her grandmother had called. She had never had a falling out

MARY GORE

with her grandmother, and she knew she hurt her feelings, but her feelings were hurt too. The phone continued to ring.

She thought of answering the call, but instead of answering she pressed ignore and waited for Rashad.

Someone knocked on her window and when she realized it was him, she jumped out her seat trying to open her door.

She hugged Rashad like she hadn't seen him in years.

"Damn Rashad who you got coming in the hood like that?" One of his homeboys said from across the street.

He turned around and told his home boy, "This my baby right here."

"Alright big dog I see you."

"Yeah you know how I rock behind mine." He said as he pulled Harmony closer. Harmony felt so safe around him, he was big, strong, muscular everything she needed.

"Come on bae lets go, I don't trust these niggas." He walked Harmony over to the passenger side of the vehicle. He opened her door, once she got in, he reached in to buckle her up.

"I need my baby safe."

She could smell the chocolate on him. Her body thumped every time she was around him. When he finally got in the driver's seat, he let the seat back, took the black from behind his ear and lit it. He put on some hood music and turned it loud. He looked at Harmony and asked her if she trusted him.

Harmony stared him in the eye and told him that she did. She had no idea what she had signed up for.

DOMESTICALLY SOUL TIED

He turned the radio up and began driving. Every time Harmony glanced at him, she felt like a little girl. She still didn't understand why she was so strongly connected to him.

She snuck another glance at him but to her surprise, he was looking at her. She clinched her thighs together. She had never felt all these feeling before.

The car stopped at the Marriott Hotel. Harmony had never had anyone to treat her and take her out like this before.

"Get out, come on bae you act like you scared," he said joking with her.

When they walked into the hotel and up to the front desk, Rashad took the lead.

"Good afternoon, sir how can I help you?" The clerk said brightly.

"Say lemme get your most expensive suite," Rashad said.

They had one available for $269 but since it was already after 12 a.m., they were willing to rent the room for $247.

As she listened to the clerk and Rashad negotiate the price, her heart melted. She had never had anyone spend this much money on her, not even her dad.

"How will you be paying?" the front desk clerk asked.

Rashad patted his empty pockets and looked at her, "Damn bae, I left my wallet in my grandma's car. When you caught that panic attack, I rushed you in the hospital and I put my wallet in the glove box! Fuck!" he yelled.

Harmony had only emergency money on her card, but she didn't want to spoil the night.

MARY GORE

"I got it bae," she said and handed her card to the attendant.

In her mind she was thinking "hope he pays me back" but it didn't matter she just wanted to make him happy. She typed in her debit card pin on the pin pad.

"Thank you, Ms. Jones room 291 is ready for you two, have fun. Checkout will be at 12:00 noon tomorrow."

They walked up the stairs holding hands. She kept going back and forth in her mind about spending that type of money on a hotel room, but when Rashad opened the door of the beautiful suite, all the second guessing stopped.

The room was lavish. It had a big living room with overstuffed couches, a full kitchen, and a big jacuzzi tub with a walk-in shower. There was a huge king size bed with roses on it.

"You like it baby?" He whispered proudly.

Harmony looked at him with adoration as if he paid for it.

"It's okay pretty fancy for me," Harmony said nonchalantly.

"Well Miss Lady, I'm about to hit this tub I'll be out in minute." Rashad said and walked into the bathroom.

Harmony waited till Rashad closed the door. She looked down and saw her phone ringing it was Iesha.

Harmony was glad she called, "Hey Iesha," she said happily.

"Hoe don't hey Iesha me, where the hell you been?"

Instead of answering, Harmony turned the camera around so that Iesha could see her plush hotel room.

DOMESTICALLY SOUL TIED

"Wait Bitch! That ain't no hospital room and it damn sure ain't no community college ain't hitting like that! Where you at?"

Harmony was waiting for the moment she could say it.

"Girl I'm with Rashad, your chocolate prince!"

"Whatever, you'd betta be safe and keep your virginity on lock tonight!"

Harmony couldn't believe her friend. She just didn't get down like that. "Girl this only my second night knowing him. Why would you think I'd even do something like that?"

"Girl I know you, but I don't know him. I love you just be safe hoe and call me asap in the morning and let me know how things went."

"Bye girl, Harmony said, "I love you too."

"Yo Harmony!" Rashad yelled from the bathroom, "Come here bae."

She got out the bed and put her ear to the door. "What do you need?"

"Man, girl come here."

She laughed and opened the door. The lights were dim, he had some candles burning, and the tub filled with bubbles.

"Come in, stop acting shy man."

Harmony walked to the edge of the tub and sat down on the side of it. She was trying to act brave, but no one had ever seen her naked. She wanted to tell him that she wasn't that

MARY GORE

type of girl, but she didn't want to make him mad, and she damn sure didn't want to seem weak.

She fidgeted talking off her clothes.

"Look at me, why you so nervous? Why do you feel like that? I'm not going to hurt you?" Rashad said softly, slowly rising from the tub.

There in front of her he stood. She immediately put her head down.

"Girl look at me," he said gruffly, "you act like you never saw a man's dick before."

"I…I haven't," she stammered, "at least not in real life."

"You haven't what?" Rashad asked disbelievingly. "So, wait you telling me you never saw a man's dick before, kissed, or touched one? Have you ever kissed a man on the lips at least?" He couldn't believe this shit.

"Nope my first kiss was yesterday when you kissed me on my forehead."

"So, wait, so what are you trying to tell me Harmony? That you a virgin or something?"

She stood there silently. She didn't want to get teased for being one.

Rashad stared at her and asked, "You are, aren't you?"

She nodded yes.

"That's why you're so special to me," Rashad said looking at her with his sexy, piercing eyes.

"What do you mean?" she asked.

DOMESTICALLY SOUL TIED

"Even though I've only been in your presence for three days, I felt you were my soul mate from the moment I met you."

"Really, Rashad?" Harmony's head was spinning. This dude really knew how to talk to women.

"Would I lie to you Harmony?"

She looked at him and shook her head no.

"Now look at me and don't close your eyes. Keep them on me, do you hear me?" he asked in a low, sexy voice, "Can you please promise me that you will keep your eyes open at me the whole time?"

Harmony was weak in the knees, "Yes, I will."

"Look at my chest, what do you see? "

Nervously, she whispered his name, "Rashad…"

"Bae, just answer." He demanded.

"You're fit, you're strong, you have abs." Harmony spoke as if she was in a trance. She was, he was putting some type of spell on her.

"Okay keep going," he coaxed.

Harmony licked her lips. She was so nervous, and she knew that he could tell.

"So, you never felt a man before?" He asked huskily.

"No, I haven't," Harmony said. She felt her panties getting moist and she instinctively knew this was what it felt like to be turned on.

MARY GORE

"Come feel me. Let me show you how a real man feels," Rashad said as pulled her to him.

Harmony hoped he couldn't feel her hands shaking as he took them and wrapped them around his long, hard penis.

She couldn't believe how weird it felt. It was hard, yet smooth and squeezable.

Rashad let her touch him for a moment then turned to let the water out. He got out of the tub and cut the shower on.

He commanded her to take her clothes off. He told her how badly he wanted to see her. As if under his spell, Harmony undressed down to her panties and bra. She was grateful Iesha had sense enough to take care of her under gear also!

"Take them off too," he said. "I want to see all of you."

When she was fully undressed, Rashad pulled her into the shower and washed her. When the hot, soapy water hit her back, he slid his hands around her and started washing her breast.

It seemed as if the soap suds were a moisturizing lotion and he was delivering a therapeutic massage. He rubbed both of her breast in opposite directions.

Harmony was trying not to bite her lips, but she couldn't help it. Rashad reached down, rubbing her belly with the towel. He washed every inch of her then turned her around to where her back faced him. Washing the front of her body, he placed his penis on her butt cheeks.

She didn't know what to do or how to stop it. She didn't even know if she wanted it to stop. She turned around on her own and looked in his eyes. The water streamed down his body and the steam of the shower made his skin shine like a candle.

She wrapped her arms around his neck. He started to softly kiss her, starting with her forehead-then he began kissing her lips passionately.

To his surprise she kissed him back as well. He pressed her body against the shower's glass doors. He licked her face, sucked on her neck, and whispered nasty words in her ear.

He turned the shower off and told Harmony to come here. She walked out the shower still dripping wet, so she grabbed a towel a dried off. She didn't understand why Rashad didn't finish. She walked in the room and there he was standing all 6'2, 225 pounds of greatness.

His penis was just swinging back and forth without him even moving.

"Do you trust me he asked?"

"Yes, Rashad yes," Harmony answered emphatically.

"Hey Alexa, play "Summer Rain".

Harmony's eyes filled with tears. "Rashad, why would you do that?" She whispered with tears ferociously falling down her face.

"Focus on me and only me," he whispered and walked over and opened the curtains. To her surprise it was raining. He walked over to her and pulled her to him.

She couldn't walk. She felt numb. Her body was weak. She hated that song and the hurtful memories it brought back. She used to love that song. Singing and clowning, performing for her father whenever it came on, now it just hurt. It brought back every memory she wanted to forget. Rashad picked Harmony up and sat her on the sofa recliner that was near the window. She looked him in his eyes and told her to watch the rain and don't watch him until she was ready to cum.

Harmony was confused. Come where? Was she supposed to go somewhere?

He spread her legs pulled her to his mouth and started to devour her. Harmony was shocked. She had heard about it, and she'd even seen a thing or two on the internet fooling around with Iesha, but she never imagined it would feel like this.

She begged and pleaded for him to stop. She began breathing faster and all she could remember was Rashad's voice saying, "watch the rain."

Tears were in her eyes when she turned to the window. With the rain falling and Rashad's tongue lavishly licking her clitoris, Harmony began to feel a sensation. She literally felt like she was leaving her body…. oh…this was the feeling that he was describing to her. She wasn't "going" anywhere. She was cumming.

Harmony grabbed Rashad's head, and he began to shake his head like a red nose pit in her. She finally for the first time in her life experienced an orgasm.

Rashad looked up and kissed the lips of her vagina then got up and got her a warm towel. He wiped her gently and went back to the bathroom.

After he brushed his teeth, he laid down in the bed with her. Harmony snuggled close and laid her head on his chest wondering why he didn't have intercourse with her. She was ready.

"Rashad, did I do something wrong?" she asked.

"No baby, why would you think that?"

"Because you didn't have sex with me."

"Harmony as bad as I wanted to, I'm saving that night for something special.

For a moment she was quiet, but before she knew it, it slipped out. Her body was speaking what her brain couldn't even process.

"I want you."

Rashad shook his head. She had come clean with him, now it was time for him to come clean with her.

"Why do you want to give your virginity to me though? I'm nobody," he said, his voice cracking a little. "My own mother didn't even want me, my grandmother hates me, I'm just fucked up…"

"I want you," Harmony firmly looking him in the eyes, "Let me be that missing piece to your puzzle."

"No Harmony, I don't want you to. I can tell you're a good girl."

"You said you're not going to hurt me Rashad, I know you won't."

He dropped his head and began tearing up, "I'm not going to hurt you Harmony," he whispered.

"Say it again!" yelled Harmony.

MARY GORE

"I'm not going to hurt you!" he repeated.

"Well come here then," she said sensually.

Rashad climbed on top of her and began kissing her softly, making every kiss count.

"You got a condom?" she whispered in his ear.

"No baby you mine, aren't you?" he asked.

"Yes baby," she replied.

He slowly took his hand and placed it on her clitoris. Rubbing it until she climaxed again. When he felt her wetness, he gently inserted his penis into her tight vagina; slowly penetrating her. She gripped her arms around his neck and held him fiercely.

As he stroked her deeply, memories of her childhood flashed before her eyes. All her years of being in school, all the hurt and pain she'd suffered-everything she'd been to up until this point didn't even matter.

She finally felt the real feeling of love. She finally felt the feeling of *being* in love. In this single moment of lust and weakness, it never dawned on her that she was losing her virginity to a guy she'd barely known a week.

She felt something wet on her cheek and looked up to see Rashad was crying. You could tell he meant each stroke as he rocked her body with his powerful pelvis.

Once she loosened up, it began to feel good and she started reacting just how he wanted her to. The more he entered the more she threw it back.

The harder he fucked her, the louder she moaned and the wetter she got. The sounds of making love to her was enough to make him explode. He tried to tell her he was about to cum, but Harmony wanted him to finish strong. She wrapped her legs around him, locked them together and held on tight. She wouldn't let him pull out, so he gushed inside of her. Rashad couldn't even move after he just rolled over and went to sleep, and so did she.

When she finally awakened, she realized Rashad was gone. She noticed a little note on the nightstand that read:

"I'll be back before checkout love you"

She immediately went to the restroom to look for her keys and purse, only to find that they were gone. She called his phone three times, but no answer. It was going straight to voicemail.

She noticed she had three missed calls from a 1-800 number that she didn't recognize. Once she called the number back it was her bank notifying her that five hundred dollars was missing from her debit card, as well as a pending transaction for $247.83 for the hotel.

When customer service asked her if she made the transactions, she wanted to say no, but she knew if she did it would get Rashad in trouble. She was sure there was some sort of explanation for this.

The representative repeated the question and told her they were calling to make sure she made them, because the card she used was only for emergency purposes.

Instead of her being honest she admitted that she gave someone permission to use her card.

"Well OKAY Ms. Jones you have a wonderful day," replied customer service and disconnected the call.

MARY GORE

She sat there in full blown tears. How could the man she just gave her virginity to steal from her and leave her stranded without her car?

The hotel phone started to ring, she jumped up to answer it hoping it was him calling.

"Hello, Ms. Jones. This is the front desk, its 11:21 a.m. and check out is at 12:00 p.m. noon. Will you be staying again?"

"Excuse me, have you seen the guy I was with last night what time did he leave?" Harmony asked frantically.

"I'm, sorry ma'am but we're not allowed to give that kind of information out."

"Please sir," she begged. "I'm only 19 years old. The guy I was with took my credit cards and car. I have no one or family up here, and besides my bank just called and told me he withdrew five hundred dollars out of my account. Please I'm begging you please tell me."

The front desk clerk stayed silent then suddenly, he told her, "All I know is around 3 am this morning, there were three other guys with him in the lobby. He was bragging about how he had hit a little sweet lick. They hung out by the pool for an hour, then we asked his company to leave for being too loud. After that, your dude called me a bitch and I haven't seen him or them since."

She immediately broke down, "I'm so sorry I know check out is noon, but can you at least give me to 12:30 p.m.? If not, I'll have to walk home."

"That will be OKAY Ms. Jones," he said feeling bad for her.

DOMESTICALLY SOUL TIED

She sat there silently, not knowing what to do or who to call on. She regretted dissing her grandma the other night.

Her phone began to ring it was Iesha.

"Hello Iesha, I can't talk right know," she said fighting back tears.

"What's wrong? I'm about to face time you and you better answer!" Iesha said before disconnecting.
Harmony tried to wipe her face before Iesha called but she could still see that Harmony was hurting.

"Tell me what happened Harmony!" yelled Iesha.

Harmony couldn't hold it in any longer. She told her everything.

Iesha stayed silent and listened to everything she'd said, but once she was finished telling her, she burst out screaming, "I'ma fuck his ass up. I got four brothers and they all did time!"

"Naw' Iesha," sniffled Harmony, "I don't want anybody to know. He took my money and my car I'm stranded at this hotel."

"Harmony, bitch you just gave this nigga your virginity and he feels like he can just take your shit because he thinks you're his."

"How can he think that?" she asked.

"Look what you just gave him!" Iesha loved her friend, but she could be naïve as hell. I wish a nigga would have pulled a stunt on me like that, she thought to herself, I would have taken the nigga's life in return. An eye for an eye in my book.

MARY GORE

She returned her focus to her friend, "Harmony, you really need to call your grandmother."

"Iesha, I can't please don't tell her this will be too much."

A private called beeped in, "Hold on Iesha, somebody calling me private."

Harmony clicked over and answered the phone.

She hears an automated voice: "Hello this is a collect call from the county jail you have a free call from Rashad Mathews if you accept please press one."

She was furious. She didn't want to accept it, but she had to.

"Hello, Harmony bae look please let me explain. I know you may hate me right now, but baby I promise I didn't take your money. Three niggas I met at that hotel last night tried to rob me after they asked me for a ride. You can even ask old boy from the lobby he will tell you."

"Rashad I could care less I want my card and my keys!" she yelled. "So, you just gone forget about me like that? I need my keys now dammit!"
"Your car is at the impound downtown. They took it when I went to jail. I already called Harmony they said it will be one hundred seventy-five dollars for you to get it out. They still got like two hundred dollars on your card though, that should be enough for you to get it."

Harmony's blood was boiling. "How the fuck you know what's in my account and how did you even know my pin number?"

DOMESTICALLY SOUL TIED

"Bae you must have forgot you typed it in last night, if I wouldn't have remembered it, them niggas would have done me in last night."

She was enraged. "Nigga bye!" she yelled before hanging up in his face.

She called Iesha back and told her to send an Uber to her location to take her to the county jail. She didn't even have time to explain to her what all he'd said.

MARY GORE

CHAPTER TEN

"Hello, my name is Harmony Jones. I came to pick up my keys out of booking for Rashad Matthews." She was irritated that the two people behind the desk were just sitting there not paying her any attention.

"Excuse me," Harmony said louder.
The guard looked her up and down and finally told her to take a seat and they would be with her shortly.

Harmony had never been in any type of jail environment. It was bad enough she still had on night clothes and a backpack. She waited a good 45 minutes before she began to get mad. Each time she saw the doors swing open and closed with no one going to get her belongings.

She watched the clock impatiently. Another day of missed classes behind the same nigga.

She decided to walk back up to the desk to ask the ladies again.

"Please ma'am I just need to get my keys and my bank card from booking from Rashad Matthews. I been waiting over a hour now."

"Do anybody have Rashad Matthew belongings so this lady can go?" The officer finally decided to show her some grace.

DOMESTICALLY SOUL TIED

Finally, they brought her the keys and bankcard. She couldn't help but to ask why he was arrested if he was the one who got robbed.

Who told you he got robbed?" The officers started to laugh.

"He did," she replied quickly.

"Well ma'am that's not what we have in our computer, but if you wait until tomorrow you can read about it in the jail docket paper. He will be in there."

"Thank you, ma'am," Harmony said as she turned and walked away with tears in her eyes.

She stood outside trying to figure out how she could get a ride to the impound without calling her grandmother.

She noticed one of the ladies from the front desk coming out the building to smoke. Harmony stood their trying not to let the officer see she was bothered or upset.

'Where you from?" The officer asked, "I can tell you're not from here are you?

"No ma'am I'm not how can you tell?"

The officer stared at her and she began to laugh.

"It's very obvious isn't it?" asked Harmony.

"My question is, how did you wind up with Ms. Diana grand boy? He ain't nothing but trouble!"

"Well, we attend the same college," Harmony explained.

"Who? Rashad?" She asked. She almost choked on her cigarette. "Girl who told you that. Rashad ain't in no damn school." She continued to laugh, "OKAY so, what's his major then?"

Harmony feeling foolish as ever said quietly, "Business and marketing, that's what he told me."

She couldn't do nothing but laugh, "Girl that boy lied the only business he got going on at the community college is marketing drug transactions and meeting females."

Harmony stood there embarrassed. It finally dawned on her that Rashad never even spoke about missing classes or studying because he never even was in one.

The officer could see that Harmony probably didn't know about Rashad's lies, and she could see that she seemed like a good girl. She hated to see her being taken advantage of.

"Look, baby you're grown, but if I were you, I would call my family and tell them the truth. That boy always had a dark past and I just don't want to see another girl be hurt. You be safe," she said as dumped her cigarette and walked away.

Harmony sat there in disbelief. She kept thinking of how everyone kept saying be safe. They obviously saw what she couldn't.

Her phone rang. It was the private number again. She answered, "Hello"

"Hey, look bae where you at?" He asked sounding like a sick dog.

"Who is this?" She wanted to make him suffer.

"It's Rashad. It sure ain't that other nigga or did you already call him up?"

DOMESTICALLY SOUL TIED

"Where are you at?" she asked ignoring him. She was annoyed that he even had the nerve to question her.

"I'm out," he said happily, "My bond was $5,000."

She looked at her phone, "$5,000? How the hell can you afford that?"

"Harmony my bond was five grand but I only paid $500 to get out."

In her mind, she knew something was fishy about this story.

"Where you at bae I miss you come here." He said sweet talking her ass again.

She couldn't believe how he was acting. Like he hadn't done shit to her. "Rashad, so you really going to pretend like you didn't steal my money and leave me at a hotel?"

Rashad was getting impatient. He tried to keep his composure. He'd messed with young girls before, but Harmony was different. She was fragile for real.

"Naw' baby, I told you them niggas robbed me."

"Who do you think I am Rashad? You just posted a $5,000 bail-I'm missing $500.00 from my account… just last night you could even pay for a room unless that was a lie too. I'm here stuck in my night clothes, can't even get a ride, and you're out of jail! You don't even care about me missing class!" she yelled.

Rashad knew she would be angry, but he didn't know she'd go off like this.

"You wouldn't care about me missing class anyway because you're not even in school!" She screamed.

MARY GORE

Rashad stayed silent until she was finished.

"You done?" He asked. "Bae, I told you I got robbed, I ain't gonna let you keep bringing this up it's either you gonna believe me or it's over."

"You really think I'm that slow Rashad? I know when a nigga running game!"

"A'ight bet! Bitch bye fuck you and them $500.00 dollars!" He hung up the phone.

Harmony was stunned. She was hurting, but she knew she had to find a way to get to her car.

She walked to the diner across the street from the jail. She glanced at the time knowing she had to get to her vehicle before the impound closes for the day and they add extra fees.

She pulled out her phone and called her grandmother.

Martha answered on the first ring. "Harmony, I've been trying to reach you. You had your grandmother worried sick."

"Hey Grandmother," Harmony said brightly, trying to make her voice sound okay. "I'm sorry Grandmother I had a long night, I need your help."

She had quickly thought of a lie. She knew if she told her grandmother what really happened, she would be pissed.

So, she made up a lie about taking one of her schoolmates' home because she needed a ride, and she didn't realize how far out it was. Then when her phone died, she parked her car in someone's yard to go find a charger at the gas station that wasn't too far away. She explained that when she returned the people towed her car because she was on private property.

"Awe, baby I'm so sorry," she said. "Tell me where you are and I'm on my way."

Harmony gave her grandmother the address to the diner and sat down to wait for her to drive from the city to her college town.

Two hours had passed when Harmony saw her grandmother pulling up. She had never been so happy in life to see her. She got into the car hoping her grandmother wouldn't get the vibe that anything was going on.

"When you started doing that?" she asked

"What Grandmother?" Harmony asked nervously. She hoped like hell her grandmother didn't have a clue as to what really happened.

Martha asked, "When did you start wearing lashes? Those are cute where you get them from?"

"Iesha's cousin Myra did my makeup the other night, I didn't even realize these were still on. They're called "Troublemaker"

"I bet," her grandmother huffed, "Beause your tail been getting into a lot of *that* lately."

Harmony started laughing, "I'm sorry for the other day, I didn't mean what I said."

Her grandmother said, "No, Harmony you were right. That boy did bring you to the hospital and I should have been grateful, but when I saw his grandmother, I just got mad all over. Mainly because she called you names and didn't even

MARY GORE

know you. She doesn't like me all over some boy. We were best friends, we hung out together every day. If she wanted Earl, I would have let her have him. I loved her not only as my friend but my sister."

Harmony looked at her grandmother and for a moment she could see she did care for Ms. Diana. "Well baby that' was then and this is now just know I love you and your grandmother is sorry."

"I forgive you if you forgive me," said Harmony.

"Done." Martha smiled, "I know your money been a little low so instead of you using your emergency cash I'll get the car out.

She was so grateful because she knew she wasn't going to have enough to make it until next semester; not with only $200.

"We here baby," Martha said handing her money, "Here's $250 that should be enough for you to get some gas, food, and pay for your towing. Are you coming by my house tonight?"

"No," Harmony replied. "I'll be over tomorrow because I have to catch up on my homework."

"Okay, baby just call me when you make it home."

After Harmony got her car out of towing, she received a text from Rashad:

"I know I fucked up big time with you and I apologize for calling you a bitch."

She didn't respond. Another text came:

DOMESTICALLY SOUL TIED

"You are a queen and I'm so sorry for that. You're a good girl, and to be honest I didn't even think you wanted to be with me. Nobody ever did shit for me growing up, the streets raised me."

She still did not respond.

Another text came through:

"So many times, I wanted to kill myself, but the thought that got me was no one would even show up."

This time, when she didn't respond, he called.

Harmony answered the phone and Rashad immediately began explaining, "Listen bae, when you were asleep last night, I wanted you to wake up with flowers, so I called my homeboy, the one you saw earlier. I found your card on the bathroom floor when I was putting on my clothes in the restroom. I put it in my pocket, because I didn't want to put my hands in your purse. You will never understand how I felt when the same niggas I was hanging with earlier pulled a gun on me. They were jealous of your car and of you baby."

Harmony knew this nigga was lying. She wanted to hang up the phone and forget she'd ever met him, but she continued to listen to his lame ass story.

"I did take your money because they had guns, but I was praying to get back to you. I fought them niggas and they ran after I gave them the money. When I sped off the police got behind me and took me to jail because the car was registered under your name. Bae it took me going to jail to see why God had us together. You my heart man; my soulmate I know you feel it come here please baby," he begged.

MARY GORE

Harmony sat in her car. A part of her wanted to hate him, but a bigger part of her knew he truly needed someone who loved him for real. He needed the one person in his life he could count on.

Against her own better judgement, she finally replied, "I love you too Rashad."

"Man, quit playing with me come here now bae I need you," Rashad said in that sexy ass voice of his.

And just like that, Harmony was back on her way to the same hood, to pick him up from the same niggas that supposedly robbed his ass.

DOMESTICALLY SOUL TIED

CHAPTER ELEVEN

"Rashad, where's your little bitch's car at?" Stella asked, standing back on one leg so Rashad could get a good look at all her thickness.

"Man, Stella stop playing with me! You know I love you." Rashad smirked. He knew she was mad cause he hadn't gave her none of that good dick in a while.

"How can you say you love me Rashad? All you do is lie and steal."

"Man, don't be talking like that in front of them like that," he said nodding towards the niggas shooting dice. "Why you call the police on me anyway?"

"Rashad you not about to be putting your hands on me. That's those other bitches you fuck with. I shoot niggas."

"Stella you my baby mama. These other hoes ain't fucking with you. You act like you don't see a nigga trying. I just want to be a family again. Can we be a family Stella?" he asked.

"Hell no we can't. Every week it's a new bitch. I'm not going to deal with this shit no more."

Rashad was so busy trying to get Stella to hear him out he didn't even hear Harmony calling him to let him know she was pulling up.

When Harmony spotted Rashad, she noticed him leaning on a car with another woman.

MARY GORE

She pulled up fast, hopped out the car and yelled in his face. "What the fuck you doing Rashad?"

"Harmony chill out!" He yelled back.

"Control your bitch Rashad before I do."

"Don't call her no bitch Stella," Rashad snapped.

"So, you taking up for this bitch now? I tell you what Rashad let that bitch take care of you go live with her. By the way don't even bother with coming to see your kids, I hate you bitch!" She yelled as she pulled off. Harmony could see Rashad was angry.

Harmony hadn't even noticed everybody standing outside looking at them.

"Get in the car and give me the keys!" yelled Rashad.

"No, Rashad who was she? And what does she mean by living with her and furthermore, what do she mean kids? Do you live with her? You told me you were back living with your grandmother!"

"Get the fuck in the car now bitch," Rashad said through clenched teeth.

Harmony got right in the car. Rashad got in the car and sped off real fast.

"Slow down!" Harmony yelled.

Rashad was enraged. He wasn't listening and he began swerving, running red lights and driving erratically over speed bumps. She looked at his face. He didn't even look like the same man she had met a few months ago.

DOMESTICALLY SOUL TIED

All she could do was buckle up for safety. Rashad pulled out a blunt from behind his ear and lit it.

"So, now you smoke weed? What else you do that you haven't told me?" Harmony asked angrily.

Rashad slammed on the brakes and looked her in the eyes and told her in the most menacing voice she'd ever heard, that she was about to find out.

"I need a place to chill for a while and think of my next move."

Harmony noticed he was driving in the direction of her grandmother house.

"Please no, anywhere but there!" Harmony yelled. She feared for her grandmother's life not knowing what he would do. She didn't want to put her grandmother in danger, so she decided to give him the location of one place she never wanted to revisit, her deceased parents' house.

Harmony put the address in for him and told him the drive was two hours away.

"Where the fuck are we going Harmony?" Rashad asked suspiciously. "This better not be no fucking setup."

"My house." Harmony said flatly.

"What house?"

"My house Rashad!" she yelled. She never wanted to tell him that she inherited a home from her father after he died but she had no choice but to tell him now.

It was the longest two hour drive she ever had in her life. It was quiet, cold, and the smell of marijuana filled her car. She felt trapped in a prison, with no chance of getting out.

MARY GORE

Rashad pulled in her father's driveway and jumped out the car. He walked over to her side ready to pull her out the car.

"Let's go," he said sharply.

Harmony unbuckled her seat belt. She was terrified of what he may do.

"What are you about to do Rashad?" She asked with tears running down her face.

How could the man she gave her virginity and trust to turn out to be the very person to hurt her?

"Let's go, I'm not going to say it again!" He yelled.

She got out the car and walked up the porch to her front door. So many emotions filled her head. Memories of her dad began to flash in her mind as she took the keys from him to unlock the door.

She paused once the door was opened. She hadn't been in the home since her father's funeral. It was like walking into a horror movie. There were spiderwebs all over the furniture and everything was dusty and smelled old.

"Bitch I said go in."

Harmony started trembling, trying her best not to have another panic attack. Rashad pushed her into the living room, and she fell on the floor in tears.

"Why are you doing this? Please! I didn't do anything."

Rashad didn't care what she was saying. He forced her to stand up and take off all her clothes. When she got down to her underwear his eyes became wild, "Hoe you must think I'm playing with you I said everything."

DOMESTICALLY SOUL TIED

"No, Rashad please tell me what I did wrong, I love you, please don't," Harmony was crying so hard she had the hiccups.

"You love me you say, so why you gonna try and check me in front of my baby mama? Now because of you I'm not going to be able to see my kids again. So, since you wanna act like a kid, I'ma show you what your daddy should of.

Rashad took off his shirt, then his belt and folded it in his hands. Harmony was standing in front of him naked and cold begging him not to hurt her.

Before she could even blink, he began whipping her with the belt, all over her body.

He started yelling with each blow, "Bitch, you took me away from my kids."

When Harmony began screaming at the top of her lungs, Rashad got even more furious.

"Bitch you trying to get the law sent over here, you trying to get me locked up?" He yelled like a mad man.

She cried and begged and swore she wasn't, but Rashad beat her even more. Even harder. Every lick stinging worse than the last one.

She tried to cover her face, but he still whipped her legs, arms, and back. How could a man, that said he loved her cause this much pain?

She stopped moving after being beat so many times. She couldn't even cry anymore. For a moment she thought the terror was over until Rashad opened her legs.

MARY GORE

He climbed on top of her. Her body was covered with lacerations and whelps. Her face was even swollen from the buckle catching her just beneath the eye from one of his swings.

He pulled his pants down and shoved his penis into Harmony. The pain ripped through her, but she was too tired to even fight back. He began humping her like he was a bear coming out of hibernation.

Her body hadn't even been broken in all the way and wasn't used to the sexual assault he was putting her through. The encounter went on for a few minutes. After ejaculating in her, he stuck his finger inside and rubbed them across Harmony's lips. She was mortified.

He gave the evilest laugh she'd ever heard and said, "Now you see who I am. Go wipe yourself off and bring me a towel."

Trembling from fear, pain, and exhaustion, Harmony eased to the bathroom and turned on the hot water.

When she sat down in the tub, the water stung her open wounds like acid. Twenty-six slashes. That's what she'd counted before losing count. She wondered if she'd lost consciousness.

Harmony looked at the medicine cabinet and for a second thought about suicide. She began to cry. She was angry with GOD. "You took my mother, my father, my best friend, and now you send me this man. I hate you!" She screamed in her soul. Not knowing that GOD was still with her.

She put her head under the water in the tub. Rashad walked in and sat on the toilet. When Harmony sat up in the tub, her soul almost left her body. She stared at him. The look on her face saying, "What more? Come on! I have nothing left."

Rashad began to cry and stared in Harmony eyes. She was so confused. Isn't this the same man that just beat the shit out of her?

"Harmony, I'm sorry," he cried. "My kids are all I got and because of you, she not gonna let me see them. I called her over there to tell her about you. That I met someone special that I love. She asked me, who? But I could tell she just was trying to be messy. Before I could text you and tell you not to come you pulled up. Harmony my mother left me with my grandmother when I was a baby. I vowed that I would never leave my kids…" His voice broke.

Harmony continued to watch Rashad's body language. The more he cried, the more he started to look like a little boy. Harmony felt her resolve slipping.

She stood up in the tub, turned the shower on, and said, "Rashad come here."

"No bae, I'm so hurt. Everybody always taking shit from me. Now I have lost you and my kids," he continued to cry.

"Come here Rashad," Harmony said. "Take off your clothes and come get in the shower."

Rashad took off his clothes got in. As he cried, he laid his head on Harmony's whelped breast. He could see what he done to her.

"I'm so sorry bae," he wept, "I'm so fucking sorry."

"Shush Rashad," Harmony cooed and pushed him to the back of the shower. She washed his body from his head to

MARY GORE

his feet. When she came up from his feet, she wiped his private area off. To her surprise, he was still crying. In the back of her mind, something said, "No Harmony." But she would do whatever it took to get him out of this mood. She replaced the towel with her tongue. "Stop Harmony!" He yelled hoarsely. His protests eventually turning into moans and groans.

With every stroke of her tongue. She looked in his eyes.

"Mmmmannn…" Rashad groaned and tilted his head back.

Harmony noticed that this was what he needed. Pleasure took his mind out of that mode. The more she sucked, licked, and massaged every area of his body, she could sense him calming down more and more, second by second.

"Come here," he said, "Your turn."

Just thirty minutes ago, he was beating her with a belt. Now he was fondling her in the shower.

The first night he made love to her, but this night he fucked her. She couldn't explain why he was so turned on and she was too. Was Harmony really that broken? Was Rashad that fucked up?

Sex was how they communicated.

He picked her up as the water hit her back. His lips grabbed her ear. He tasted her neck taking his tongue licking her face. Harmony tilted her head back as he pushed his nose against her whelped breast-sucking them like she just gave birth to him he needed milk.

He took his tongue and went around and around throwing, her head against the shower door.

DOMESTICALLY SOUL TIED

When Harmony looked him in the eyes, he said, "Choke me."

"What Rashad?" She couldn't have heard him right.

He said, "Bae choke me, and hit me."

Harmony choked and slapped him.

"Now put your nails in my back," he growled. Following his every instruction, Harmony began to power up. All she could think of is how he beat her downstairs with that belt, how he'd lied to her repeatedly, how she never got her money back…. she gave him what he wanted.

He screwed her all the way to her bed. He told her to turn over and spread her legs. His tongue pleasured her private. He devoured her insides and Harmony began begging him to stop.

"Please bae, please bae, I can't take no more" she moaned.

"You really want me to stop?" he asked. "Do you really want Daddy to stop?"

When he said "Daddy" her eyes popped wide open and she realized how fucked up she was. While he was busting inside her, tears began to flow from her eyes.

"How could I?" She thought, "In my own parent's house? He just beat me. How did we wind up having sex when I was just laid out on the floor? How could my body be turned on to that sick madness? Why did my body enjoy it?"

She fought with her own thoughts back and forth. When Rashad rolled over and had fallen asleep, Harmony rolled over and cried.

MARY GORE

CHAPTER TWELVE

Harmony's voice mail notifications were going off. She
awoke feeling sore and stiff from the night before and
headed in the bathroom to brush her teeth and listen to her
messages.

She heard the sweetest message from her grandmother.
How badly she wanted to run into her grandmother's arms
and tell her everything. She wanted to hear her
grandmother's strong, reassuring voice telling her that
everything was going to be alright.

But instead, she had to deal with the monster that the man
she loved had turned into.

She took a quick shower, quietly dressed, and slipped out
before Rashad woke up. As soon as the cold air hit her, she
realized that she had forgotten her jacket, but she didn't
dare go back.

She wanted to run and get some things for breakfast and
figure out how to get out of this mess.

She noticed she needed gas, so she stopped at the nearby
gas station.

"Can I get $30 on pump four?" she asked.

Harmony didn't recognize Mr. Samuels, who used to be her
dad's best friend.

"Harmony is that you?" He asked, happy to see her.

DOMESTICALLY SOUL TIED

"Hey Mr. Samuels," she answered.

"Come give me a hug. I haven't seen you since your dad's funeral," Mr. Samuels said grabbing her in a bear hug.

Harmony winced in pain and he looked down and said, "Harmony, you're bleeding."

She hadn't even noticed the lashes were slit to the white meat.

He asked her what happened, and Harmony made up a lie about rescuing a wild cat that scratched her. Mr. Samuels knew it wasn't true, but he didn't want to pressure her.

Harmony turned around to leave, anxious to get away from Mr. Samuels. She walked right into the person coming in through the door.

It was Stella. Rashad's baby's Mama. What a freaky coincidence.

"Oh, so you the bitch Rashad wants.

"Do I know you"? Harmony asked, knowing full well who she was.

"My name is Stella bitch. I'm Rashad's wife."

"Look, I'm sorry," Harmony said, she was shaking badly. Stella looked right at her arms and noticed the lashes.

Almost immediately, her demeanor changed. "Look baby girl, you need to leave Rashad, that," she said pointing to Harmony's arms, "THIS is why I left him alone. He has a dark side."

MARY GORE

Harmony said, "Rashad told me that you're just trying to break us up. He told me he was trying to tell you he wanted me, and you were mad."

"No baby," Stella said. "He called me there because he pulled up at my house in your car at five in the morning telling me he had wanted to take me out to breakfast. I went. He drove straight to the ATM machine and withdrew five hundred dollars. While he was getting the money out, I was looking around in the car. I saw your dad's obituary in the glove box. I remember reading about your dad in the newspaper because that story made me cry. When I picked up the insurance card, I noticed your name. I said to myself, "I can't do this". I politely told him to take me home. He got mad and tried to put his hands on me, I called the police. Yes baby, he was in jail because of me."

Harmony dropped down to her knees. Mr. Samuels ran outside of the gas station and said, "Harmony are you okay?"

"What is wrong with her?" Stella yelled. "I didn't do nothing to her!"

Mr. Samuels replied, "She suffers from anxiety attacks. Run get some cold water for her."

Stella did just that. After Harmony began to calm down, she overheard Stella telling Mr. Samuels, "You know I wasn't trying to hurt Harmony, but Rashad gone really wind up killing someone and I don't want it to be her. She's young and has already went through so much. I got to go now. Please Mr. Samuels, tell her not to tell him I told her and if she doesn't believe me tell her to call and ask where he was picked up for that night and what were his charges."

DOMESTICALLY SOUL TIED

"I'm calling your grandmother," Mr. Samuels said helping her to her feet.

"Mr. Samuels no. Please I'm okay," Harmony said.

Mr. Samuels walked Harmony to her car and sat down in the passenger seat to make sure she was okay to drive. She asked him to reach in the glove box and hand her the medication that was inside.

After she took her anxiety pills and drank water, she started feeling better.

She looked over at Mr. Samuels and asked, "Can you call the police department to check to see why Rashad was picked up and what was his charges?"

Mr. Samuels shook his head and answered, "No Harmony, just leave him alone."

"Please Mr. Samuels, do this for me. I need to know." Harmony pleaded.

Mr. Samuels grabbed Harmony's phone and called the police station. He'd had a friend that worked in the intake department. "Hey Officer Stacy," Mr. Samuels said, greeting his friend.

"How can I help you brother?" Officer Stacy replied.

Mr. Samuels said to Officer Stacy, "Look bro, you know I don't ever get in anyone's business, but I need a favor. You know Diana's grand boy? The one that broke in my store a few years back?"

"Yeah, what did he do now? That boy stays in trouble," Officer Stacy replied as Harmony listened in shock.

MARY GORE

The phone was on speaker so there was no mistaking what she heard him say.

Mr. Samuels asked, "What did he get arrested for yesterday?"

Officer Stacy told him to hold on a second. You could hear the clicking of his computer keys, then he responded, "He got into an altercation with his baby mother. She called the police stating he tried to spend money on her, and she knew he was up to something. She then gave us the description of the car he was driving. We pulled him over. He gave us the wrong name. So, we towed the vehicle and locked him up for giving false information."

"Thanks Officer Stacy," Mr. Samuels said. "What was his bond amount?"

Officer Stacy replied, "One moment let me see."

Mr. Samuels could see how hard this was for Harmony. "Hey Sam, are you still there?" Officer Stacy asked.

"Yes," Mr. Samuels responded.

Rashad bonded out on a five-hundred-dollar bail paid in all twenty-dollar bills.

"Thanks bro, you are the best." Mr. Samuels thanked Officer Stacy for the information about Rashad and hung up.

Harmony began punching the dashboard and screaming. She had never known this type of life nor had ever dealt with these types of people.

Mr. Samuels knowing nothing else to do to calm her down, called her grandmother.

DOMESTICALLY SOUL TIED

"Hello Martha," Mr. Samuels said quickly.

"Who is this calling me from Harmony's phone?" Mrs. Martha shouted.

"This is Darren Samuels; I own the gas station remember? I was your son in law's best friend. Your granddaughter needs you."

Mrs. Martha responded quickly, "What happened? Is she alright?"

"No. It's something to do with that Matthews boy," Mr. Samuels replied.

"I'll pay you if you can bring her to my house. I'm on my way home but I have to make one stop, then I'll meet y'all at my house."

"Yes Ma'am, anything I can do to help this family out, I will do it."

Thank you, Darren, now tell Harmony her grandmother is on the way."

Mrs. Martha grabbed her bat and put on her tennis shoes, then she headed out the front door of her home.

MARY GORE

CHAPTER THIRTEEN

Rashad woke up and looked around for Harmony. He saw the note she left him saying she was going to grab them breakfast.

He got up to look around the house. When he walked in her parents' room, he saw all the beautiful pictures of Harmony's mother. Damn! He saw where baby girl got her looks from. He saw where she got those eyes from.

On the dresser there was a brown music box. He remembered his mom had one that played ballerina music. He opened it and saw two diamond rings and a gold Rolex watch. He looked around to make sure no one was there.

If only he knew the trauma that he caused Harmony by stealing her mother's engagement and wedding rings and her father's gold Rolex that he received from his wife on their first wedding anniversary.

He got dressed and headed out and at the same time, clear across town, Martha was pulling up to Rashad's grandmother Diana's house, with a bat.

She banged on the door with the bat and shouted, "Open up bitch! Open up!"

Diana opened her screen door with a cigarette in her hand. "Why are you here? And what do you want?" Diana yelled.

"What did your grandson do to my granddaughter?" Martha demanded.

DOMESTICALLY SOUL TIED

"I don't know. He hasn't been home in the past few weeks." Diana explained.

Martha yelled, "If he did something to Harmony, I'm whooping his ass."

Diana blew smoke in her face and said, "You been gone out of the hood for too long cause a bat ain't gonna do shit to a gun. You just need to leave."

Martha walked up to the screen door and said, "David slayed a giant with a rock. What makes you think, I'm scared of a gun?"

"Like I said Martha, leave. Please!" Mrs. Diana said with a frighten facial expression. Just then, she noticed Rashad running up the street yelling "Grandma who's at the door?"

Diana begged Martha to leave quickly. For the first time Martha could see the fear in Diana eyes. "

"I'll call you please hurry and go!" yelled Diana. Martha almost tripped trying to get to her car before Rashad made it to the house. By the time she pulled off Rashad was standing in the street with a gun pointing at her way.

"Rashad get in here!" yelled Ms. Diana, "Where have you been anyway?"

Rashad looked like a mad man. You should have let me shoot that bitch!" He yelled, ignoring his grandmother.

Diana continued to try and calm Rashad down. She explained that Martha and she had bad blood ever since she took Earl from her.

MARY GORE

Rashad reached in his pocket and pulled out a wad of hundreds, "Here there you go," he said pushing the money toward her.

Diana couldn't help but to wonder where he got that money from.

"What did you do Rashad?"

"What you mean Grandma?"

"Baby this woman come over here asking about her granddaughter, you been missing for days, and now you come giving me hundreds, something aint right."

"Just take the money!" He yelled.

"No, Rashad, I can't take it," Martha said handing him back the folded bills.

"Well fuck it!" He exploded. "You been on my ass about helping you out around the house now I'm trying to help you and you say no?"

Diana took a deep breath and stood her ground. She didn't want to hurt him, but he needed to hear the truth.

She yelled, "Rashad I can't take this anymore! I have watched you steal, beat women, sell drugs, and do prison time. I can't do it anymore. I've tried to raise you right."

"Raise me?" He yelled, "All you ever did was remind me of how my bitch ass mama didn't want me, how you could have enjoyed your life if you never would have taken me in. Man bye, the next time you see me make sure your church hat is fixed nice and proper because you'll be at the front row of my funeral. You know how you don't want them church ladies talking about you."

DOMESTICALLY SOUL TIED

Diana put her head down and wept bitterly. Deep down she knew that although she'd done the best she could with this boy, she had failed him.

By the time Martha made it to her house, Harmony was there. She hugged her granddaughter tightly and immediately noticed the lacerations on her arms.

She couldn't do nothing but cry. Mr. Samuels said, "I'll leave you two alone. Harmony I think you should tell your grandma everything."

Mrs. Martha looked down at Harmony then at Mr. Samuels wondering if she'd missed something.

She and Harmony went into the house and sat on the sofa. Harmony poured her heart out. She was hesitant at first and kept looking at her grandmother's face to see if she was judging her.

All she saw was love and support, so Harmony told her everything, even about having sex with him after he beat her.

For the first time throughout the conversation, Martha was shocked, and before she could help it, she blurted, "You had sex with him after he beat you? "How could you?"

Harmony was hurt. How could she be truthful with people if they were going to get mad at her truth?

"Never mind," Harmony said, jumping up abruptly. "I can take care of myself."

Harmony walked quickly to the car and started her engine. Martha stood in the doorway with tears in her eyes. She knew it just as sure as anything.

MARY GORE

Her granddaughter was in a deeply dysfunctional domestic violent relationship. She was domestically soul tied.

Harmony drove with tears in her eyes. She was tired. Tired of arguing and fighting with the people she loved. When she arrived back at her parent's house, she felt unsure of what she would walk into.

She walked up the steps opened the door and called out to Rashad. "Rashad are you here?"

No one answered. She walked up to her parent's room and sat at the foot of the bed and cried. She held her dad's pillow, smelling his scent and remembering how he used to smell so good after he shaved in the mornings.

She screamed loudly into the pillow but stopped suddenly when she noticed the top to her mother's jewelry box was off.

She stood there in shock and in disbelief. She stood over the jewelry box and peered inside. The remainder of her heart shattered.

Her mother's wedding and engagement rings were gone. Harmony picked up and held the empty jewelry box in her hands yelling, "NO! NO! NO! NO!"

She gripped her heart and fell to the floor. Even her dad's favorite watch was missing. Everything that was left to her from her parents was gone. Although her mom had been gone all her life, her dad's death was still fresh. It had only been four months. Harmony had never felt such monstrous rage. Right there on her parents' bedroom floor, she finally let out all the pain she'd been holding in.

DOMESTICALLY SOUL TIED

CHAPTER FOURTEEN

"Hey Myra. This is Iesha. Have you heard from Harmony?" Iesha asked, glad that Myra answered the phone. Lately, she had been to herself.

Myra told her she hadn't seen Harmony since she'd gotten her together for her date. When Iesha told Myra, she hadn't seen or really heard from Harmony except to send her an Uber to pick her car up from jail, Myra knew she had to tell her.

"Iesha, I didn't want to say anything, but that boy is no good. Everybody at the school know him. He screws anything that walks, and he got a reputation for beating women. The last girl he beat so badly, she had to go to a shelter four states over."

"How you know Myra?" Iesha asked.

"Because the girl he beat was me," Myra respond. "I never knew it was Rashad she was talking to because when I glanced at the phone, she had his name saved in her contacts as Ronald, but I knew his voice immediately. I never forget a voice."

"Why did you come back Myra and what if he saw you? Iesha asked, still not wanting to believe her.

"I came in for only two days to visit my mom." said Myra. The day when you called me to make-up Harmony's face, you made me smile. I used to love doing hair and makeup, so that really made my day. I was having a wonderful time

MARY GORE

but when I heard his voice, I left immediately. You never forget a voice.

"I'm so sorry Myra," Iesha said.

"It's okay, I'm healing, doing better, and my baby is too."
"Baby! What baby?" Iesha shouted.

Myra responded, "When I left five months ago, I didn't know I was pregnant. He doesn't know either and neither does she so don't tell her. Harmony wouldn't be able to handle it."

"I love you cousin," Iesha said.

"I love you too. Bye girl," Myra said, her voice trembling.

Iesha just sat there in stunned silence trying to decide on what to do. As much as she loved college, she knew her friend needed her. She went and told the administrator that she needed three days off due to a family emergency. Once she got approved, Iesha was on her way.

A few hours later, Harmony woke to the sound of loud knocking. She had cried herself to sleep holding her mother's empty jewelry box.

"Harmony are you there?" Martha screamed through the door. Pulling out her spare key, Martha turned the doorknob and walked in with two police officers. When Harmony heard her grandmother's voice, she was too weak, drained, and exhausted to even say anything. She couldn't move. She just moaned.

Martha and the officers rushed in the room and picked Harmony up from the floor. Mrs. Martha told them that Harmony needed her medicine.

DOMESTICALLY SOUL TIED

As she rumbled through the medicine cabinet Martha noticed that Harmony hadn't taken her medication in months.

"Does she need an ambulance?" the officer asked.

"No. She just needs a moment."

After taking her medication and thirty minutes of fanning, Harmony started to feel better. She was finally stable enough to talk.

The officers explained to her that they came so that they can get a statement from her to press charges on Rashad.

"Wait. What?" Harmony asked, shaking her head.

"Yes, your grandmother told us everything, we're going to get you in a battered women's shelter. You need to put him away. This same guy has beaten up three other women. One woman just five months ago. That woman is in a shelter right now fearing for her life."

"Well, why isn't he in prison?" Harmony asked.

"Because the women are scared of him." the officer responded.

"So, you want me to put my life in danger when they didn't?" Harmony asked incredulously. "I'll take my chances."

"Look Ms. Jones, we understand your position and place in all of this. We can even omit the fact that you had sex with him after he had beaten you. We can say he forced you to have sex with him."

MARY GORE

Harmony went from shock to rage. She looked at her grandmother and growled with her fist close tight; "How could you tell these men what I did?"

"She was trying to help." said the officer.

"Help by telling strange men all of my business? That's not no help. If I have never hated you, I hate you NOW!" shouted Harmony.

"You can hate me all you want, but I never beat you like Rashad did."

The officers got between them and asked Martha if she could step out.

Mrs. Martha growled, "No. Why? I'm the one that called you. She needs to put him in jail."

The officer turned and asked Harmony how old she was. When she told him he was 19, he told Martha that he would only be able to speak with Harmony if she was willing. He handed his card to Harmony and he and his partner walked towards the door.

The officers escorted her grandmother down the stairs. Before they walked off, Harmony called out to the officer, looking at him with such sadness in her eyes and asked him, "Do you have any kids?"

"Yes. Yes, I do. I have two girls," he said.

"How old are they?"

"One is seven and the other one is three."

She then asked, "Is their mother around?"

"Yes. Their mother is my wife," he answered.

DOMESTICALLY SOUL TIED

Harmony said softly, "Well my mom died after I was born, my dad died a month before my high school graduation, and the only boy that truly loved me died next to my dad on the same day. Now, the guy you are talking about is a monster. I thought he loved me. I thought he really did love me," she said as she broke down in tears.

Although the officer was on the duty, he hugged Harmony and she cried in his arms. The officer could see that she needed to feel the love of a caring father.

"Look Harmony, as bad as I want you to press charges on this guy, it will do more damage than helping you if we try to pressure you to do it. You need time to heal, baby girl. I knew your father. He sold me my SUV. When I told him my wife was pregnant, I remember he told me about his daughter named Harmony and she had eyes like sunflower. He told me about how he would play song called "Summer Rain" every day for you, because it made you smile. I didn't like the SUV at first, but the way your dad smiled when he talked about you-well, it made me buy that SUV. That was seven years ago, and my daughter Melody loves it."

She couldn't hold back the tears. "I miss my dad so much. I disappointed him. I MESSED UP," she wailed.

"Harmony, you can still make it right," the officer said. "If you don't stop Rashad, who will? Rashad has been bad news all his life, but he messed up when he put his hands on someone that was cared about and loved by many people. I'm not speaking negatively against the other women, but Harmony take your life back." The officer pleaded with her mournfully. She sat there for a moment and said. "I would like to file charges."

MARY GORE

CHAPTER FIFTEEN

Iesha pulled up to Harmony's parents' house and saw the police cars. She reached for her gun and puts it in her purse. She ran in the house yelling, "Where that fucking nigga at?"

The officers stopped Iesha and were questioning her when Harmony yelled down that she was good.

"I'm up here Iesha. I'll be down in a minute," she yelled.

The second officer finished taking Harmony's report, handed her a card, then told her they'll contact her in the morning. They also told her not to have any contact with Rashad. Harmony asked the officer if they could do one more favor. She asked them to escort her grandmother off her property.

Martha was crushed. With tears in her eyes she told Harmony, "Really Harmony? I done all this for you, and you send me away? Okay, fine I'll leave, but you remember this."

Harmony stood there with tears in her eyes while the officers escorted her grandmother to her car.

By then, Iesha was walking up and screamed out, "Don't worry Ms. Martha, she just needs time. She'll call you."

When she saw the look on Harmony's face, she was speechless. In all the years she'd known her, she'd never seen Harmony this angry.

DOMESTICALLY SOUL TIED

"What is wrong Harmony?" Iesha cried out. "What did he do to you?"

Harmony dropped her head and began to cry uncontrollably. "He stole my mama's ..."

"What?" Iesha said. "I can't hear you girl."

Harmony shouted, "Iesha he stole my mama's rings and my dad's watch."

Iesha knew how much those items meant to her friend. "Aw' fuck that, this nigga gone get smoked," Iesha shouted and pulled out her gun.

"Where you get that gun from?" Harmony asked.

"It's legal," Iesha answered, "I don't trust him Harmony. You need it more than me," Iesha said and handed her the gun.

"I can't, please Iesha." Harmony pleaded with her.

"Man, this punk stole from you and beat you. Plus, he beat my cousin Myra, left her pregnant and alone. This mother fucker needs to die." Iesha uttered violently.

Harmony replied, "Wait! What?"

Iesha was so enraged she couldn't control herself. She slipped and told Harmony about Rashad's last victim being her cousin Myra.

Harmony said, "What cousin?" "What baby?"

Iesha shook her head and told her, "I just found out, damn man."

"Tell me please, I need to know."

MARY GORE

"My cousin Myra that did your make-up, she didn't know that the guy you were seeing was Rashad because you saved his number as Ronald. She was just dating him. He beat her badly and she ended up in a shelter for battered woman. She found out she was pregnant and didn't tell him; and she wants to keep it that way."

Pissed off more than ever, Harmony told Iesha, "Give me your gun."

"No Harmony!" Iesha yelled.

"Iesha, I am going to get that jewelry back. That's all I got left of my parents." She begged Iesha for the gun.

"Harmony just let the police handle it please," said Iesha.

Harmony looked at Iesha and said, "You said it! He beat three women already and I was the fourth one. He will not hurt another woman. If going to jail didn't change him, I can." Harmony said earnestly.

"NO Harmony," Iesha pleaded. "We can find another way to get the jewelry. You are not me. You don't need a gun; you were not taught this way."

Harmony looked at her friend and said, "It's funny. All it takes is a weak ass nigga to grow a person up overnight. Now give me the damn gun."

DOMESTICALLY SOUL TIED

CHAPTER SIXTEEN

Diana pulled the crumpled paper from the kitchen drawer, looking for the phone number she vowed to never call.

She dialed the number, and a voice answered on the second ring.

Diana couldn't breathe for a second, "Hello."

"Who is this?" the voice said.

"MaryAnn this is your mama. I know you can't talk long, but Rashad is really in a bad place. You been in hiding too long baby, that man is gone, and your child needs you.

"Mama, I swore to you I'd never come back." said MaryAnn. "I know I hurt you so bad. I wanted to give Rashad the best life, but I couldn't take no more beatings."

"I know baby," replied Diana, "but your child needs you. He has wronged so many people. He might not make another day.

"Mama please, he's okay," MaryAnn said. Her mama was probably being over dramatic, wanting her to come home.

"Now MaryAnn, I took care of your child for twenty-five years. I watched him punch walls, fight his boys, beat on women, and even use guns to kill. You don't even know how scared I was too live with him. He doesn't respect me or others. You got a chance to run away from his dad, but Rashad is his son. When his dad died you should have

MARY GORE

come back, but you didn't. Now I'm old. I can't take this dysfunction anymore. Get here now and save your child."

After hanging up the phone, MaryAnn turned to hear little feet walking up.

"Mommy who's that?" A beautiful, bright eyed little girl asked.

"Your grandmother; my mother," MaryAnn said quietly.

"I thought you said your mom was dead?"

MaryAnn began to cry.

"Daddy" Her daughter Alina yelled, "something is wrong with mommy!

Her husband rushed in to find his wife in tears and his daughter looking worried. He asked her what was wrong.

MaryAnn cried, "It's my son. It's my mother. We must get to them now. I'll explain on the way."

Rashad had no idea what was about to happen.

"Hey Rashad, word around town is that chick with the black car pressed charges on you," one of the hood chicks yelled down at him from her raggedy project screen door.

"Quit playing!" Rashad yelled back. "Who told you that?"

"Call the station and ask they will tell you dummy!" She said and quickly shut her door. Bitches knew better than to talk crazy to that maniac.

At first Rashad thought that ho was playing but he called down there anyway just to see if it was true.

DOMESTICALLY SOUL TIED

"Hello, is this the police department? My name is Rashad Wallace." Before he could ask his question, a gruff voice said quickly, "Yes sir, you need to come on in and speak to a detective involving a incident that took place earlier."

"Is this about a chick named Harmony?" Rashad asked innocently.

"Sir, I'm not at liberty to say…"

Rashad had already recognized the voice, "Officer Stacy I know this your fat ass don't forget who I am. Now I'm going to ask you again is this about her?"

"Yeah Rashad. Listen young man. I went to school with her father. Her father was a good man. He had done a lot for a lot of people in this community. He loved his daughter, man."

Rashad wasn't trying to hear that shit. He put his phone on speaker and said, "One last thing OFFICER STACY…"

Just then the sound of crunching glass scraping cement and loud stomping noises could be heard through the phone line.

"Rashad," Officer Stacy asked, "What the fuck was that?"

"You tell that snitching bitch I said fuck her dad, and this cheap ass watch."

That's when Officer Stacy realized it was the same watch Edward used to brag about all the time because that was the last gift his wife gave him. This nigga Rashad was just ruthless man.

MARY GORE

Iesha was in the kitchen cooking Harmony some food when Harmony's phone rang. The person on the other line asked to speak with Harmony.

"This is she," Harmony said.

"This is Officer Stacy. I know you were with Darren Samuels when he called earlier. You need to find a safe place to be until we can get you placed in a shelter. We think Rashad is spiraling out of control. He took your dad's Rolex watch and smashed it on the ground. If he didn't value a watch that cost as much as his grandma's house, he's not going to value your life."

"Yes sir. I have a girlfriend here with me now. We are going to her brother's house who lives outside the city," Harmony lied before hanging up the phone.

She looked at Iesha's purse laying on the sofa. She saw the gun's handle hanging out and she grabbed it. She was filled with white rage and anger. She was just a bomb waiting to explode. With the gun in hand, she walked out the door.

Iesha didn't even realize Harmony was gone until she went looking for her phone. She saw she had two text messages that read:

"The motherfucker smashed my father's watch"

And:

"I'm going to kill that nigga"

Iesha broke down in tears, ran and looked n her purse, and realized Harmony had stolen her gun. All she could think was that boy just stole all her mother's jewelry, her daddy watch, not only that he beat the girl this morning with a belt. Iesha grabbed her purse and keys and headed out the door dialing 911.

By the time she made it to Ms. Martha's house, she was a nervous wreck. Hours had passed and there was still no word from Rashad or Harmony. Iesha had called and told Ms. Martha while she was on her way about what Rashad took from her. As they waited for the police, they could only imagine how Harmony was feeling.

When the police arrived, Martha informed them of Harmony's state of mind. She explained that Harmony hadn't taken her meds in months and this type of situation could make her explode. She didn't know how she could handle all those emotions.

The officers advised them that Harmony may have just needed some time to cool off and would probably come back home. They told her if they didn't hear from her by the morning, they would start looking for her.

Ms. Martha and Iesha agreed.

MARY GORE

CHAPTER SEVENTEEN

Ms. Diana woke up to several knocks at her door. She opened it to find her daughter MaryAnn standing there with a cute little girl and a nice-looking man.

"MaryAnn is that you?" She asked.

"Yes, mama it's me."

They hugged tightly for a long moment and she finally welcomed them in to be seated.

MaryAnn took it all in. She hadn't smelled these familiar smells in ages. The musty smell of her mother's old furniture mixed with the smell of mothballs and fried food filled the air.

Nothing had changed, MaryAnn could feel all the feelings she tried avoiding coming back to her.

Her mother noticed the look on her face and explained, "Well baby, after you left it seemed like time just stopped."

"Mama I'm so sorry, I didn't mean for none of this to happen. This is my husband Lamar, and my beautiful daughter Diana Alina."

Her mother was shocked, "Did you say Diana?"

"Yes, mama I named her after you."

Diana was momentarily speechless. Finally, she asked, "Is she really your daughter?"

DOMESTICALLY SOUL TIED

"Yes, mama she's nine years old. I didn't want to tell you, because I didn't want you thinking I didn't want my son. I kept this from not only you, but I kept my past from my husband also." She stood up and continued in tears, "I owe all of you the truth, I can't keep in any longer. Twenty-five years ago, I met my abuser. He practically beat me every day and night like a dog. I never could understand why he was so evil because when we met, he worshiped the ground I walked on. Between alcohol and drugs, he hid his addiction from me until he couldn't hide it anymore. I wanted to leave so badly, but then I found out I was pregnant with Rashad. I thought things would get better, but when I had Rashad it got worse."

Everyone listened intently. MaryAnn's husband and daughter were in tears listening to the woman they love share her pain.

She continued, "The day I gave birth to Rashad, his father became impossible to handle. He choked me in the delivery room, because I was crying from the pain of afterbirth."

Diana couldn't hold it in any longer. Tears streamed down her face as she cried, feeling like the world's biggest failure.

MaryAnn persisted with her story, "When I made it back from the hospital to the house he didn't like the attention I was giving Rashad. One day he pulled Rashad out of my arms because I was singing to him. It got worse by the day. At first, he would just stare at me and Rashad, then he began abusing me again. He even threw Rashad on the floor and when I went to grab him, he started kicking me and biting me. The last straw was when he forced me to have sex with him and my baby wasn't even a week old.

126

MARY GORE

That night I decided to pack a bag for two people, but it wasn't for Rashad to come with me. I knew eventually his father would take his anger out on him. I hated to leave my baby, but he was better of being safe and loved than to be with me. I dropped Rashad off that morning to you mama, because I knew you would keep him safe. I lied to his father and pretended that I didn't want the baby. I convinced him that I just wanted him, to my surprise he believed me. He told me he was driving us to Vegas so we could get married real fast. I knew that was my only opportunity to run far away. I waited until we were about 40 miles out from there, I told him I had to use the restroom. He pulled over to the gas station and when he wasn't looking, I ran as far as I could. When I finally arrived at the police station, I told them I didn't have no family or no anyone I just needed help. They sent me to a domestic shelter for help. Five years later when I heard about his dad passing, the first thing I did was call home. I called and to my surprise Rashad answered, and when I told him who I was, he told me that I wasn't his mother, that his mother was dead. That's the day I decided enough damage was done. I tried to protect him by leaving, but that turned out to be the worst thing I could have done. On that day I asked God to forgive me and I wanted to serve him. I always prayed for my son, and for God to give me another chance at real love. A year later I met Lamar. I sent you money every month hoping that he would have the best of clothes, and the best things, but now I know most of all he needed me, and I wasn't there for him." She broke down.

Her husband came over and assured her that he forgives her for not telling him. Her daughter curled up on her lap and told her what a good mommy she's been, and Diana held her head to her breast and let her cry.

DOMESTICALLY SOUL TIED

CHAPTER EIGHTEEN

Out of the blue Rashad entered the room in a rage. "So, this what we doing now?" He stood there with a gun pointed at his own mother's face.

Diana begged him to put the gun down.

Rashad wasn't listening. Instead he said, "Like I told the bitch on the phone that day my mother is dead to me."

Lamar stepped in front of his wife and pleaded with Rashad, "Son your mother has been through so much, please we can talk about this."

Rashad aimed at Lamar's head and told him, "Nigga you don't even know me! You don't know how it feels for someone to remind you constantly of how your mother left you and ran off with a nigga. Do you Mr. Armani suit?"

Lamar looked him right in his eyes and said, "No I don't, but if you were my son, I would have hugged you, sat you down and talked to you, told you how sorry I was. I can still be that father figure to you, but you have to put the gun down."

Just then they heard a car slam on its brakes. Rashad still had the gun pointed on Lamar and MaryAnn when suddenly Harmony burst through the door yelling, "I know your bitch ass is here, Rashad!"

MARY GORE

She stopped in her tracks when she saw him there with the gun pointed at a man and a woman. She'd already had Iesha's gun out and down and her side.

She immediately pointed at him.

Diana was crying and begging for them to drop the guns while holding her granddaughter behind her for safety.

MaryAnn pushed Lamar and stood between Rashad and Harmony.

"You really want this smoke huh?" yelled Rashad now pointing the gun at Harmony and his mother. Lamar jumped up and begged MaryAnn to stay out of it, but with tears running down her face she turned and looked at Harmony.

Harmony nervously held the gun shaking, she pointed the gun directly at MaryAnn. "Please move or I'm going to have to shoot you too."

MaryAnn could see the hurt, fear, and rage in her eyes. She understood the feelings Harmony felt. I was just like you before I met Rashad's father. Harmony looked at MaryAnn closely and could see the resemblance to Rashad.

"You're his mother? That nigga told me his mother left him and was dead, another lie!" Harmony yelled and cocked the gun.

"Wait!" MaryAnn yelled, trying her best to keep the attention on her. "His dad used to beat me, he would kick, punch, spit and do so many awful things to me. The sad part is that I allowed him to. I thought that was all I deserved. That all changed when I found out I was pregnant with Rashad." She turned around and stared in his eyes. "I found out what real love is. It doesn't hurt or hit you. It doesn't curse at you, or steal from you, because love something real and special, baby I was broken before I even got with your dad. I was molested by my own father as a young girl. A man who was supposed to love me and protect me, not me. I couldn't even tell my mother because she loved her perfect husband."

Diana hung her head in shame. She suspected Earl had done something to this girl, but she was so hell bent on not letting Martha win him back, she guess she just blocked it out.

MaryAnn tried her best to plead with both Harmony and Rashad to put their guns down.

Harmony was still shaking. The man with the gun, was looked more and more like the little five-year-old boy who only needed love. She could tell he was at his breaking point.

Rashad look at his mother and screamed, "You hate me because I'm just like him, don't you?"

"No baby Rashad, I love you, we don't have to repeat this cycle you can change I can get you help. Put the gun down baby please…"

Just as Rashad was about to put the gun down, six officers burst through the door with their guns drawn at Harmony and Rashad. Harmony could hear Iesha and her grandmother outside yelling and screaming.

MaryAnn pleaded with the officers to let her talk to her son, but the officers yelled again for them to put down their weapons.

MARY GORE

Harmony, who still had the gun pointed at Rashad yelled at him, "Why couldn't you just love me? You knew I was broken; you took everything away from me I had. I gave you my virginity, I let you in my parents' home and you stole from me." Harmony aimed her gun more in his direction

Rashad broke down in tears. "I did love you. I wanted to play you, but I couldn't. But I couldn't let you go either. There's just something that takes over me that I can't control. I wasn't trying to hurt you intentionally. I'm just truly fucked up."

The cops screamed their last warning. MaryAnn and Diana beg for Rashad to put the gun down, Iesha and Martha begging for Harmony to put hers down.

"Please let me just talk to my son!" MaryAnn cried.

For the first time, Rashad *felt* her when she said those words. It was almost as if he were hearing them for the first time.

With his attention diverted, the cop decided to end it and fired several rounds into Rashad's body.

Blood splashed across Diana's and Lamar's faces.

"No!" MaryAnn wailed and threw herself across her son's lifeless body.

Harmony turned to the officer that shot Rashad and aimed the gun at him.

"No, Harmony!" Yelled Mr. Mark, the cop who hugged her like a father earlier that day.

DOMESTICALLY SOUL TIED

Harmony's life flashed before her eyes. She saw images of her mother and memories of her father flooded her mind. She remembered her father driving her to school, and Eric smiling at her. She looked at Rashad's mother crying and saw the blood coming from Rashad's body.

She dropped a tear and pulled the trigger, barely missing the officer.

A total of six shots hit Harmony, before she dropped to the floor. She didn't have anything or anyone to live for anymore. She felt being dead was better than being alive. She looked over at Rashad as she took her last breath and whispered, "I love you."

Iesha and Martha ran over to where Harmony lay, and they were both crying hysterically. All Martha could think is how her entire family had been taken from her.

When the ambulance pulled in and the emergency crew rushed in, they checked the pulse of Rashad and pronounced him dead on the scene. When they checked Harmony's pulse to their surprise it was faint, but she was still breathing. They carried her out on a stretcher and placed her in an ambulance.

Martha could fill the presence of God even in the midst of the hell that broke through. Iesha couldn't believe that she was still alive because when she'd felt Harmony's chest there was no heartbeat. She couldn't do anything but say God thank you.

MARY GORE

CHAPTER NINETEEN

The coroner placed Rashad lifeless body in the black bag.
A letter dropped out of his pocket, and MaryAnn
immediately picked it up. Her husband told her, he had to
get her mother and daughter out the house and he would be
back once he got them to safety. MaryAnn told him it
would be okay. She headed upstairs in a daze and went into
her mother's bathroom. She sat on the toilet and held the
letter that her deceased son wrote. She read the letter
although it was addressed to Harmony.

Dear Harmony,

*I know you hate me right now. I hate myself also. I know I
met you a few months ago, but it seemed like destiny. From
the first time I saw you smile; I knew you were different.
You never asked me for anything. You gave me love even
when I didn't show it to you. That night at the hotel, I made
love to you like I never did in my life. I let the wrong people
influence me. I saw your bank card, and I checked your
balance.*

*I did go straight to my baby mama crib because I wanted to
get some things for my kids, but like her she threw up my
past in my face. She was thinking I was on some sex shit,
but really, I just wanted to be finally able to give her what*

DOMESTICALLY SOUL TIED

*she deserved. I saw her as a good mother, I fucked that up,
but when I met you. I wanted to have something out of life.
I put my hands on you, and I saw your heart break before I
ever even had a chance to fix it. I whooped you like you
was a dog on the street. I took the jewelry, because I felt
you already had a lot. I was selfish it was like a demon took
over me or something. We bonded quickly because of or
issues. I took the money back to the pawn shop and got
your mothers rings. I know this apology is too late, but just
know this Harmony I really did love you even when I didn't
love myself. Gods going to send you someone and when he
does, don't hate him because of me. Allow him to love you
Queen because that's what you are. I paid and got your
mothers rings cleaned for you, love you I'm so sorry.
Rashad.*

MaryAnn couldn't do anything but cry. She looked inside
the envelope and the two rings were there.

She felt cold and old. She never thought about how her
leaving him affected Rashad, or what it could do to a child
to go through so much tragedy and pain. Now she realized
that if children don't grow up with the love they need, they
turn into selfish, sick adults.

She headed to the hospital in hopes that Harmony was
okay. When she arrived, she ran into Ms. Martha and Iesha
in the waiting room area. When Ms. Martha spotted her,
she immediately started cursing, asking why she would
come here. MaryAnn understood why she was mad, but she
had just too lost her son as well.

"Look I know you hate me, but your granddaughter needs
help. I left over twenty-five years ago leaving my son,
because I was running away from my problem. Rashad's

MARY GORE

father beat me every day, I was molested by my father, I need to help her because if that baby doesn't get help, she will be in jail, or dead."

Martha looked at her and asked if Earl was her father and MaryAnn broke down in tears.

Ms. Martha gave her a hug and said, "I tried to tell your mother when we were in school that boy was bad, but she wouldn't listen, thinking I was hating her or something. Baby I'm so sorry."

They hugged as the doctor approached them with the news that Harmony was going to be OKAY. The doctor told them that she was shot twice in her legs, twice in the shoulder, and one bullet had grazed her arm. The one that hit the left side of her chest pierced her lung.

"We did surgery, but she will be okay," the doctor concluded.

Martha said, "Thank you Jesus!"

"Can we see her?" Iesha asked impatiently.

They were told only two at a time because she was still in ICU. MaryAnn asked Ms. Martha would it be OKAY for her to see to Harmony alone after they saw her. She agreed that it would be OKAY.

MaryAnn waited on her turn to see Harmony. Visions of her son kept popping up. She prayed that God would give her strength in this time. Ms. Martha finally came out the room to let MaryAnn know she could see her but warned her that Harmony was not responding and couldn't speak.

Before MaryAnn entered the room, she noticed two officers sitting guard. She walked in the cold dark room; all she could see of Harmony was her face. Everything else was wrapped up in bandages. She sat along the side of the bed and pushed the chair as close as she could.

MaryAnn could see Harmony eyes lids blinking, so she placed her hand on Harmony hands.

"Harmony, this is Rashad's mother. I know you can't speak but if you can understand me squeeze my hand."

For a moment she thought it was useless and she started to cry. Out of the blue Harmony, squeezed her hand. MaryAnn was so happy, she asked Harmony if it was okay to read something from Rashad to her.

Harmony squeezed her hand again. MaryAnn pulled out the letter and began to read it. Word after word tears began falling out her eyes. One she got done reading her the letter Rashad wrote, she placed her two mother's rings in her hand.

Harmony began to cry more and squeezed her hand. MaryAnn stood up and touched Harmony's forehead and told her, "I may not have known my son, but I know love when I see it. Being soul tied to someone is unpredictable. It happens quickly, he saw you coming from a mile away. Your brokenness attracted his. I never thought I would see my son take his last breath, but his last words when I bent down to hug him, he whispered he loved you. This will take a long time to get over, but God has you just like he has me. Your grandmother will never understand why you loved him, but I saw it in your eyes that you in fact loved my son. If he never done nothing right in his life, this letter showed me that although his daddy was in him, so was I." She kissed Harmony on the forehead and left the room.

MARY GORE

EPILOGUE

One month after Harmony got out of the hospital, she still had to go on trial to face the charges from the day Rashad passed. Although the officer didn't get shot, she still had to plead her case for attempted capital murder.

Her lawyer explained to the judge about Harmony's state of mind and he even showed the hospitals records stating that she wasn't taking her medication. He argued that if she was, she would have been able to make more rational decisions. With the passing of her mother, father, friend, and all the things she went through with Rashad, he gave her 100 hours of community service, one year of counseling and ordered her to be reinstated on her medicine.

A year after Rashad's death, Harmony and his mother started an outreach program for domestic violence, but also for those who suffer from childhood trauma.

They believed if someone could have talked to Rashad and Harmony as kids and worked with them on their issues individually, Rashad wouldn't have lost his life, and Harmony would have never been able to fall for Rashad so quickly.

Not only women, but there are men that could lose their life to domestic violence, but also for others that try to support them like Edward, Eric and his siblings.

DOMESTICALLY SOUL TIED

As Harmony looked back, she saw where she went wrong. Covering up your past or hiding real issues can only lead you further away from help.

Ms. Martha and Ms. Diana became back good friends. Iesha went back to school to finish as a psychologist.

Mr. Lamar, and Rashad's sister Diana joined the outreach group also, but most of all, Harmony finally found herself, and her true purpose.

Domestic Violence is never okay. If you or someone you know is being abused:

Call the National Domestic Violence Hotline

1-800-799-7233

MARY GORE

DEDICATION

First, to God: I want to thank you for giving me the courage and understanding to finally see what my purpose in life was. You gave me the strength to endure going through my storm. You allowed me to not only come out with sunlight, but the choice to go help someone come out as well.

To my beautiful boys: Jamory, Emon, Nolan, and Eauxrion. Y'all have watched me for years deal with verbal, mental, and physical abuse, and yet through it all y'all never gave up on me. We went from house, to apartments, to a domestic violence shelter, but your mother finally got it right. I love y'all so much.

To my mother Pandural: You gave me the strength to believe in myself. When people reminded you of my past, you steadily defended my past, present, and future. When I look for the definition of a mother it's still not enough to define you.

To Kevin,Alex and Donna: I have to say thank you ya'll for a true definition of a blended family.

DOMESTICALLY SOUL TIED

To my big sister Theresa: I love you and your strong words that I needed and when I needed you, you were always there.

To my family, my besties: El and San, Tina, Tyuana I love all of you.

To Lawernce: Thank you for always telling and reminding me who I am.

To Agbona: Thank you for making my vision come to life.

To Ms. TiTi: Thank you for giving me this chance. When everyone turned me down you came back for the underdogs and gave us a seat at the table now, we can all eat.

To Barbra Gore: I love you.

MARY GORE

Author Mary Gore was born in New Orleans,
Louisiana where she lived until hurricane Katrina
hit and relocated to Mississippi. There she attended
West Jones High School and where she later
graduated.

Mary attended Delgado Community College where
she majored in Criminal Justice. She's had various
jobs in the criminal justice field and has been a
correctional officer, armed guard, police officer,

private investigator, and now she is a director in a corrections facility.

She is a single mother of four beautiful boys.

Mary's goal is to help others who are going through abusive relationships find a way out, such as she did.

She feels that whether you are going through domestic violence in a relationship, fighting addiction, or anything else that hinders you from operating in your highest capability, there is hope.

Made in the USA
Monee, IL
04 September 2020